Slocum drew fire with his hat, sprinted for his Appaloosa. He vaulted into the saddle, stayed low and rode at a gallop. As he neared the pines, he drew his six-shooter. But he didn't slow his attack. If he had, he would have provided a decent target. Bursting into a grassy clearing, Slocum wheeled around, expecting to see someone pop out to take a shot at him.

Silence. Slocum felt the hair on the back of his neck ripple. No white man crept about in the forest this quietly.

With his head to the side he heard the sound of distant horses. It sounded like a half dozen or more ponies—an entire hunting party. Slocum holstered his six-shooter and drew the Winchester from its saddle sheath. Guiding his Appaloosa using only his knees, Slocum lifted the rifle to his shoulder when he saw shadows. Cocking the rifle produced a sound that echoed through the still forest. He fired in one smooth motion. Venting a bloodcurdling rebel yell, he plunged through the undergrowth and fired left and right.

When his six-gun came up empty, he headed back toward Ella.

"John," she gasped out. "D-did you kill whoever was shooting at us?"

As he slowed, Slocum looked around to be sure he wasn't blundering into a trap. His mouth went dry when he saw crossed lances thrust into the ground.

"This is an Indian burial ground," he said. "Sacred earth."

"Dr. Marsh is going to be so happy. It's a new dinosaur find," Ella said.

"We can't go back there. It's desecration."

"Oh, bother," she said. "Dead's dead. Isn't that what paleontology is all about? Bones?"

"Those are human bones back there."

DON'T MISS THESE
ALL-ACTION WESTERN SERIES
FROM THE BERKLEY PUBLISHING GROUP

THE GUNSMITH by J. R. Roberts
Clint Adams was a legend among lawmen, outlaws, and ladies.
They called him . . . the Gunsmith.

LONGARM by Tabor Evans
The popular long-running series about Deputy U.S. Marshal
Long—his life, his loves, his fight for justice.

SLOCUM by Jake Logan
Today's longest-running action Western. John Slocum rides
a deadly trail of hot blood and cold steel.

BUSHWHACKERS by B. J. Lanagan
An action-packed series by the creators of Longarm! The
rousing adventures of the most brutal gang of cutthroats ever
assembled—Quantrill's Raiders.

DIAMONDBACK by Guy Brewer
Dex Yancey is Diamondback, a Southern gentleman turned
con man when his brother cheats him out of the family fortune. Ladies love him. Gamblers hate him. But nobody pulls
one over on Dex. . . .

WILDGUN by Jack Hanson
The blazing adventures of mountain man Will Barlow—from
the creators of Longarm!

TEXAS TRACKER by Tom Calhoun
Meet J. T. Law: the most relentless—and dangerous—man-
hunter in all Texas. Where sheriffs and posses fail, he's the
best man to bring in the most vicious outlaws—for a price.

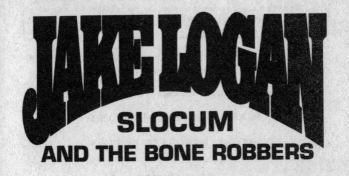

JAKE LOGAN

SLOCUM
AND THE BONE ROBBERS

JOVE BOOKS, NEW YORK

SLOCUM AND THE BONE ROBBERS

A Jove Book / published by arrangement with
the author

PRINTING HISTORY
Jove edition / January 2004

ISBN: 0-515-13658-1

A JOVE BOOK®
Jove Books are published by The Berkley Publishing Group,
a division of Penguin Group (USA) Inc.,
375 Hudson Street, New York, New York 10014.
JOVE and the "J" design
are trademarks belonging to Penguin Group (USA) Inc.

PRINTED IN THE UNITED STATES OF AMERICA

10 9 8 7 6 5 4 3 2 1

1

The Wyoming grassland stretched flat as any Nebraska prairie, but John Slocum hardly noticed the persistent oceanlike ripples in the knee-high grass or the occasional deep ravine cut by spring runoff a few months earlier. His eyes fixed on the towering mountains to the west, their snowy pinnacles almost lost in purple haze. It had been too long since he had wandered through the rocky expanse, enjoying the high meadows, the cool, clear streams and, most of all, the feeling of freedom. For the past three months, the lanky six-footer had been in St. Louis amid crowds that jostled his elbows, pushed and shoved and made more noise than he cared for.

Slocum might have left the bustling city earlier, but he had felt obligated to stay until his friend Marcus Lawson was properly planted in the ground and resting easy for all eternity. Lawson had run afoul of a back-shooter, so Slocum had taken it upon himself to be certain that the gunman never put another notch on his six-shooter.

Tracking the smallish, rat-faced man down had taken longer than Slocum had expected because of the St. Louis crowding, but he had done it. The fight had been fair, Slocum facing the man when he drew and fired. From the gunman's slowness on the draw, Slocum doubted he had ever killed anyone other than by shooting him when his back was turned. It hadn't pained Slocum one bit to see the man flop over and fall into the Mississippi River, to be swept away by the powerful current. Unfortunately, the law hadn't seen eye to eye with him that he was simply doing their job for them. He had left the river port in a hurry and was now glad that he had.

A stiff, almost chilly breeze blew off the mountains. Probably a branch of the Wasatch, Slocum figured, not that it mattered one whit to him. Brisk, clean air carrying the odor of things growing—he smelled more than that. He smelled freedom again.

Then he heard carried along on the wind a faint metallic noise that sent him diving to his left from his horse. Barely had he nosedived from the saddle when lead ripped savagely through the air. He had missed being shot from the saddle by a fraction of a second.

Slocum landed hard on the ground and lay still for a moment, gathering his wits. His horse, a sturdy Appaloosa, bolted and ran, neighing in fear. Slocum shifted his weight slightly and scanned the immediate terrain. Since the sound had been carried on the wind, that meant the bushwhacker lay ahead and probably to his left, in a shallow ravine.

Lying still only invited a shot that might do some real damage, but Slocum had to find where the no-account snake was hiding before he could return fire. He slipped his Colt Navy from the cross-draw holster and cocked it. To him the sound was like a cannon firing, but he knew his attacker couldn't hear what was actually a faint noise. Not only was the man upwind, but Slocum's six-shooter was well oiled and virtually silent in operation until it spat leaden death. Only Slocum's heightened senses made the noise out to be the peal of doom.

His lips curled back in a feral snarl. The peal of doom

would sound, all right—for the son of a bitch trying to shoot him from ambush.

Slocum had poked his head up a mite, hoping to catch a glint of sunlight off a rifle barrel, when he thought he had been thrust back in time to the war. Bullets raced back and forth and smoke obscured the once-empty Wyoming sky. He had been in battles during the war with fewer rounds than this being fired. He flopped onto his belly and got his bearings. If he was going to survive, he needed cover.

Wiggling across the grassland caused in the knee-high gray-green buffalo a constant ripple grass that couldn't be obscured, but Slocum thought finding a safe arroyo was more important than not betraying his progress. A new barrage drove him flat onto his belly again. The very air reeked of gunsmoke now, as white clouds drifted over him on the mountain breeze.

He wondered what he had ridden into. The bullet that had almost killed him was probably meant for someone else—and that someone else was returning the shot with a vengeance multiplied tenfold. From the rapid fire, Slocum guessed there were a dozen men shooting at each other. Whatever the feud, it wasn't his.

Crawling across spiny weeds and cutting himself on rocks that poked up, he managed to get into an arroyo more than deep enough to allow him to stand. He leaned against the loamy bank. Aggrieved noise from farther up the arroyo brought him around, six-shooter level and ready to fire. Instead of shooting, he holstered his pistol and whistled loudly.

This produced a new round of gunfire. It also brought his Appaloosa trotting back down the sandy-bottomed ravine. Slocum swung into the saddle but kept his head low as he urged his horse to remain in the arroyo. The steep banks provided ample protection from the still-raging battle until he was a quarter mile away. Only then did he trust himself enough to sit upright in the saddle and crane around to see if he could catch sight of the combatants.

An occasional muzzle flash was the only clue he had as to the location of the men so avidly shooting at each other. He put his heels to the Appaloosa's flanks and got the horse to a trot. By the time the arroyo had petered out, he was far enough away from the gunfire to hear only distant echoes slithering across the grassland like frightened snakes. He tried to get his bearings, since he wasn't certain where he was. Less than fifteen minutes of riding away from the gunfire brought him to a well-travelled road angling toward the mountains.

He wasn't inclined to seek out the company of men, not after the set-to back in St. Louis, but he needed a shot of whiskey to wet his whistle and to settle his nerves. He also needed to know who was so determined to kill a pilgrim out on the prairie—so he could avoid the man.

Fort Bridger, he decided. He was heading toward the old mountain man's trading post. Slocum had never met Jim Bridger, but the fur trapper's reputation bordered on legend. Slocum didn't have much truck with living legends, but he saw no other direction in which to head.

Now and then he cast a glance to his backtrail, making certain the men so intent on ventilating one another weren't after him. By the time he saw the trading post, shadows stretched across the land and a few gas lamps at the post were being lit. He rode up slowly, taking in the rough-hewn patrons. The glory days of the trapper and fur trader were long gone, the European appetite for beaver and fur hats history. But these men looked prosperous enough, as well as a tad on the disreputable side. Slocum reckoned they hired themselves out as hunters for any of the U.S. Army posts scattered around, and maybe even as guides and scouts. Ever since '73, life had been hard all around. The biggest railroads had gone belly-up and had taken most of the country with them when they defaulted on their railroad bonds, but a few Eastern tourists still came to Wyoming to shoot buffalo and to pretend they were roughing it.

"Howdy, mister," called a burly man dressed in buckskins. He pushed open the creaky door of what passed for a saloon and stepped out to greet Slocum. "Come on in and have a drink. Firstun's always on the house."

"Much obliged," Slocum said, swinging down. He was a bit sore from his rapid unseating from his horse back on the grasslands.

"You been travelin' long? You got the look of a man about fixin' to fall apart." The man stared at Slocum from under bushy brows, his gray eyes keen and not missing a detail.

"Not that long today, but I almost got myself drygulched out on the prairie. Couldn't have been ten miles from here."

"Do tell," the man said. He spat into the street and looked disgusted. "I wish them fools'd jist kill each other and not try to take everyone else with 'em."

"A range war?" guessed Slocum.

"Not exactly, though we've had our share of that in the past. You lookin' for a job?" The man spat again, then took another bite off the tobacco he carried wrapped up in his dangling leather pouch.

"Just passing through," Slocum said. He looked around the bar and felt right at home. He had seen a dozen—a hundred—like it all over the West. Behind the bar, between two cracked mirrors, stretched a languid nude painted onto what looked like a wood plank. She had long, flowing red hair that barely hid her pulchritude and did nothing to diminish her come-hither expression.

The bar was stained by too many spilled beers, and ankle-deep sawdust on the floor soaked up what was spilled there, be it beer or blood. A piano was propped against the back wall, but no one sat on the decrepit stool to play it. A dozen tables, some with card games going, were spaced throughout the large room. At the rear of the room two men played billiards.

"What's yer pleasure, mister?" the buckskin-clad barkeep asked as he agilely vaulted the bar, landing lightly behind it.

"You said something's free. I'll start with that," Slocum said. The bartender poured a fierce-looking liquor into a shot glass that was surprisingly clean. Slocum knocked it back, felt it kick like a furious mule, then put down the shot glass on the bar.

"Another?"

"Why not?" Slocum said. He had tasted worse.

"You got the look of an experienced cowhand about you," the barkeep said. "Old Mathiesen out on the Triple Cross is lookin' for range hands who know one end of a lariat from the other."

"You recruiting for him?" asked Slocum, swallowing hard as the tarantula juice hammered into his gut.

"Always on the lookout for the folks round the tradin' post," the barkeep said. "The more what come to work here, the more of 'em I'll see here swillin' my whiskey. Pretty durn good, ain't it?"

Slocum nodded. He didn't trust himself to speak, not for a few minutes, until the forest fire blazing in his throat died down a mite.

"I make it up out back." The barkeep looked harder at Slocum, then said, "I kin use a bouncer. You got the look of a man able to use that piece of iron dangling at your hip."

"Just passing through," Slocum repeated.

"Did I hear Luke say you were looking for a job?"

Slocum turned and looked at a man dressed roughly in homespuns. But there was something that alerted Slocum. The clothes might be those favored by a scout but the face was too full, too soft. The skin wasn't turned to leather by long hours in the sun and wind. If anything, there was more than a hint of peeling from sunburn on the forehead. This man, maybe in his early twenties, didn't belong on the frontier as much as he did somewhere back East.

"No," Slocum said.

"You a gunfighter?" the man asked, almost timidly.

"No." Slocum turned to leave. He'd had his pair of drinks. That was plenty. He dropped a dime on the bar. Luke snared it before it stopped rolling around on its rim.

"Wait, sir. We can use a man like you." The young man grabbed Slocum's arm.

Slocum jerked free, turned and squared off. The coldness in his green eyes caused the man to step back a pace.

"Didn't mean anything by it. We need scouts. We need men who can fight."

"Because you can't?" Slocum asked.

"That's right, sir," the man said, color coming back to his face. He warmed to his sales pitch. "My employer is none other than Professor Othniel Marsh, of Yale University." He saw this meant little to Slocum. "In New Haven, Connecticut. You have heard of this esteemed center for higher education, have you not?"

"I have," Slocum allowed.

"Then you realize the professor would only pursue the most important of scientific expeditions. He is the foremost paleontologist in the world."

Slocum had heard of Yale. He had no idea what a paleontologist was.

The man didn't notice his lack and rushed on with his spiel. "We can pay ten dollars a week, plus a bonus should you find a worthy dinosaur skeleton. Why, if it is special and no one else has found one like it, the professor might name it after you! After he had properly identified it, that is."

"Not interested."

"But, sir!"

Slocum left the saloon, not wanting to listen to another word. In his hurry to leave, he bumped into another man, one who might have been the twin to the one inside the saloon. The only difference was in the way they were dressed. This one wore fancy Eastern-style duds, now the worse for wear and hanging in dirty tatters in places.

"I heard you turn Sanborn down. Good," the man said. "That leaves you free to come work for Mr. Cope."

"Who?" Slocum wondered if everyone at Fort Bridger was as crazy as a loon.

"Mr. Edward Drinker Cope. Surely, you have heard of him! He is from New Jersey and is the world's foremost—"

"Paleontologist," Slocum finished.

"Why, yes, that is so. You *have* heard of him. His fame is secure due to his discovery of the elasmosaurus in a New Jersey marl, but he is not one to let moss grow under his feet, not at all! He wants to discover new species of—"

"Dinosaur," Slocum interrupted again.

"Yes, yes! You will make a splendid addition to Mr. Cope's party. When can you come to our camp and begin work?" The man's eagerness bothered Slocum. The man's hot eyes gleamed with a hint of fire. Or was it insanity?

"Let me guess," Slocum said. "Your side and the other—the one led by Professor Marsh—were shooting it out earlier today."

"Out on the prairie, why yes, we were. They tried to steal our bones! We were defending not only ourselves but our discoveries. Marsh is infamous in academic circles for stealing the discoveries of other, better scientists."

Slocum snorted and turned his back. He had heard enough craziness. These Easterners were free to kill each other, and they could do it without his help.

He swung up into the saddle, wondering how far from the trading post he could get in the twilight, before he had to stop for the night.

2

Slocum kept riding in spite of the inky darkness. The stars overhead came and went behind wisps of clouds blowing in from the west, casting the entire range into a night so intense he could hardly see the ground at times. A brisk, increasingly cold wind blowing off the distant mountains added to the feeling this wasn't the right time to be riding. A storm might be brewing. He knew he should go to ground, find shelter, sleep and ride on refreshed in the morning, but he wanted to put as many miles between him and the feuding professors as he could.

That's what he wanted but it was not what happened. Less than an hour away from Fort Bridger, Slocum heard a calf lowing piteously. He drew rein and slowly turned until he located the sounds coming from a ways to his right. The clouds broke apart and let enough starlight fall on the prairie to give him a fair look at the land. Mostly grassy, but scarred with deep ravines cut by swift runoff from melting snow in the mountains every spring.

The calf's anguished cries grew louder and more insistent. Slocum wasn't the kind to let an animal suffer. He wheeled his Appaloosa about and started for the distressed calf, slowing when the sounds got more piercing and he still couldn't see it.

Puzzled, Slocum dismounted and tethered his horse to a sturdy rabbit bush. He walked forward slowly in the dark and was glad he had been so cautious. The ground fell downward suddenly into a murky pit, causing him to scramble back. He grabbed wildly as he felt his boots slipping down the slope into the hole. His fingers closed on a clump of buffalo grass, tightened and held. The roots began pulling free, but by this time Slocum was kicking and driving his toes into the soft dirt to gain a foothold on the pit wall. He finally got enough traction to propel himself from the hole.

Rolling over and sitting up on solid earth, he saw that the ground had simply opened up into a pit almost twenty feet across. The calf at the bottom continued its soul-tearing wails, but Slocum wasn't as inclined to rescue it now. Not until he got a better look at the sinkhole. He edged forward until he could look down the steep side to where the calf fought valiantly and futilely to escape.

"Just like an ant lion," he muttered. In Texas, he had seen sandy pits dug by small insects. A curious ant came by, slid down and then had the side of the conical depression constantly dug out from under it by the ant lion until exhaustion set in. Then the ant lion emerged from under the sand and dined.

Slocum doubted any such insect had dug this pit. More likely water running underground had hollowed out the entire subterranean area. The water dried up, and the calf came along and had been heavy enough to cause the bubble of hardened mud to collapse.

Slocum knew he should wait until dawn to try getting the calf free—even smarter, he knew he should ignore the animal's plight. This animal wasn't his property. But he couldn't let the frightened calf remain in the pit, especially if a storm came whipping through. The pit would fill and possibly drown the animal. Even if the storm petered out, from the way the calf fought, it would either die of exhaustion and fright or cause the side of the pit to fall in on it, like an ant lion's trap.

"Just you calm yourself," Slocum said in a level voice, hoping his words soothed the animal. "I'll get you out somehow."

"What'll you do then?" came a raspy voice.

Slocum spun, hand going to his six-shooter. He froze when he saw that the cowboy behind him held a leveled rifle.

"I wanted to get the calf out before it killed itself."

"You a rustler?"

Slocum had to laugh. "Now that's about the stupidest question I ever heard. If I am, would I admit it to a man holding a rifle on me?"

"Reckon not," the cowboy said, lowering the rifle. "You actually intended to free the calf? Not butcher and eat it?"

"I've got plenty in my larder," Slocum said. "Salt pork and bacon's not the same as a tender steak, but it'll do me."

"We've had a dozen or more of these pits open up across the ranch," the man said, passing Slocum to peer over the edge at the calf. "Dangedest things I ever did see. Almost wish the dirt wasn't soft so that the spring runoff didn't dig down like that."

Slocum had guessed right about the cause of the pit.

"How do you usually get your livestock out?" Slocum asked.

"Don't usually find 'em in time," the cowboy said, resting the rifle barrel across the crook of his left arm so he could thrust out his right hand. "My name's Chafee. I ride for Mr. Mathiesen."

"The Triple Cross," Slocum said. "The barkeep at Fort Bridger mentioned it." He introduced himself.

"Pleased to make your acquaintance, Slocum. Mr. Mathiesen's about the best owner to work for in these parts, but there's not a whole lot of men willing to work right now."

Slocum heard something else in Chafee's words. He stayed quiet and let the cowboy ramble on.

"Truth is, Mr. Mathiesen's running the spread short-handed 'cuz of gold strikes up in Idaho. Nobody wants to earn a fair wage when there's a fortune to be had digging metal out of the ground. I stayed on, more out of loyalty than good sense, but he needs experienced hands to work the herd." Chafee cast a gimlet eye on Slocum. "You looking for work? Can't pay as much as a silver strike up in Virginia City, but you'd get three squares a day."

"Let's get the calf out of trouble. Then we'll talk." Slocum wasn't sure why he said that. He was hightailing it across Wyoming for Utah and had no reason to stay. The feud between the professors was only part of it. The more distance he put between St. Louis and his back, the more he'd relax.

Slocum and Chafee spent the next three hours getting ropes around the calf, hog-tying it and then dragging it up the steep side of the pit. When Slocum yanked off the rawhide strips around the calf's legs, the critter jumped up, tried to kick him and then raced off into the night just as the storm hit.

"So much for gratitude," Slocum said, dusting off his hands and pulling back his rope, forming the lariat into a loop to fasten on his saddle again. He pulled up his collar against the rain and tugged at the broad brim of his hat to keep the water from his eyes.

"Even if you don't stay on as a ranch hand, let me stand you to a good breakfast. For this much work, you deserve it. Mrs. Mathiesen's a right good cook. Fact is, she's the best this side of the Platte. It'll let you dry out a mite, too. No other place but the Triple Cross ranch house for shelter within ten miles."

Chafee rambled on about this and that, more to hear the sound of his own voice than to amuse Slocum. They rode to the ranch house in a light drizzle, arriving as the gray-haired Mrs. Mathiesen put out the best table Slocum could remember.

Somehow, in the middle of his third helping of eggs, he agreed to hire on. With such good victuals riding in his belly, Wyoming seemed plenty of distance between him and his woes with the law back in St. Louis.

"Don't know how a bunch of herd animals can have such minds of their own," mused Chafee. "Wasn't a couple weeks back, we had most of them in for branding. Now they're scattered to the four winds. Some of the mamas took their calves with them, and we might have missed putting the Triple Cross on their hides."

"I'll ride toward the mountains," Slocum said. "I might find a few in that direction."

"I'll go parallel to the north. If you don't find nuthin' by midday, you hie on back."

"I wouldn't want to miss the noon meal," Slocum said with a smile. "But I'm not as familiar with the country as you. It might take a bit longer."

"Then get your carcass back by dinner," Chafee said. "That'll leave that much more of Mrs. Mathiesen's fine corn bread for me at lunch." With a laugh, Chafee rode away at a trot. Slocum thought hard for a minute, wondering why he had agreed to stay. The owner's wife put out a fine spread but he had never thought with his belly. He looked around and knew why he had decided this wasn't such a bad place to spend the summer.

Cool wind whipped down from the high country, rustling through knee-high grass. A man could get to like this wild, wide-open land. More than that, he had hit it off right away with Chafee, as if they had been partners for an entire season. The others at the Triple Cross were also likable enough, if a bit standoffish, but Slocum had come to trust Chafee. He couldn't say that about many men.

Slocum heaved a sigh and started riding steadily for the distance-hazed mountains, still capped in the purest white. He kept his eyes peeled for any strays, especially heifers and calves that might have escaped branding, but the only animals he saw were rabbits, wolves and the occasional bullsnake slithering from one shady spot to another as the sun worked its way up into the sky.

The breeze in his leathery face and the sun on his back, he rode toward a stand of cottonwoods where strays might go to find a watering hole. He smiled when he heard a cow lowing, followed by a loud slurping sound as it drank. Slocum couldn't see the pool of water or the cow, but his instincts had been right.

He slowed his approach when he saw a saddled horse impatiently tugging at its reins securely tethered to a distant tree. Slocum knew that Chafee was always on the lookout for rustlers. A gang working on this open range might account for Mathiesen's beeves being scattered from one side of Wyoming to the other.

Slocum reached over and made certain his Colt Navy rode easy in his cross-draw holster, then advanced. From his position astride his horse he got quite an eyeful.

A delightful eyeful.

The cow he had heard munched at juicy grass near the pool, but coming straight up from the surface of the pool, as naked as a jaybird, rose a true vision of feminine beauty. She wore her auburn hair cut short, almost mannishly, but there any comparison with a man ended. Skin so white it gleamed like alabaster in the morning sunlight, ample breasts, firm and high-placed, narrow waist and flaring hips—very definitely female.

Slocum's Appaloosa whinnied and drew the woman's attention.

"Anything else, besides your spying eyes, riding up all high and mighty?" she asked. She made no effort to hide her nakedness. Slocum saw the coppery plains around her nipples, now taut like spring berries from the cold water.

"Sorry, ma'am," Slocum said, touching the brim of his floppy black hat. "Didn't mean to snoop. I'm out running down strays. Like that one yonder." He never took his sharp green eyes off her, nor did she seem to be a bit shy about her lack of clothing.

"Well, I never!" she snorted. She slapped one hand down on the surface of the water and sent spray flying like tiny diamonds into the air.

"You never what?" Slocum asked.

"I've never been so insulted!"

This surprised him. She was wantonly showing him her naked feminine charms and making no effort to hide modestly.

"Sorry."

"You certainly are sorry if you hadn't intended spying on me. What sort of men do they have out here on the frontier?"

"I don't follow you."

"Don't you *want* to look at me? What's wrong with my body?" She took a step out of the water, the waves lapping around the bottom of her finely turned rump and revealing the fleecy nest of reddish hair nestled between her legs.

"There's nothing wrong with your body. I could look at it all day long," he said honestly. Slocum couldn't figure her out.

"See!" she cried, coming from the water to stand on the bank clad only in water droplets and sunlight. "You could stare at me all day, but not all night! Am I so ugly, then?"

"You're the prettiest filly I've seen in many a year," Slocum said, beginning to understand. "You're so pretty, I don't understand why you think you have to fish for compliments."

This brought a laugh to her ruby lips. She tossed back her head and sent a curtain of water cascading from her short, wet hair. "I seem to be surrounded by men who put politeness ahead of voicing what they really think," she said, turning boldly to face him.

"Right now, I can't say what I think. My brain's a bit befuddled by your beauty," Slocum said, "but I surely do know what I want." He dropped to the ground, swung the Appaloosa's reins around a low tree limb and went to where the woman stood.

She was taller than he had thought, maybe as tall as five-foot-six. He used his extra six inches of height to look down into twinkling eyes so blue they shamed the sky. He took her in his arms and planted a juicy kiss on her lips, almost expecting her to cry out.

"That's more like it," she said softly. "At last, a real man." She ran her nimble fingers down the front of his jeans, then let out a gasp of delight. "A *real* man, from the feel of it."

He discarded his gunbelt while she worked to free the buttons at his fly.

"Definitely a real man from the look. And the taste," she said before her mouth was occupied in a more delightful fashion.

Slocum went weak in the legs when her red lips closed on the tip of his manhood. Her tongue lashed out, licking and stroking, teasing and tormenting until he shifted his weight from foot to foot. He reached down and put his hand on her wet hair, then guided her back and forth in a rhythm that sent electric tingles into his loins.

The woman pulled away and looked up at him, smiling wickedly.

"Tasty," she said. "But you weren't looking for me. What brings you out here?"

"I told you. I was looking for strays. Reckon I found me one."

"Indeed? Are you good with that rope?" She turned a little to look in the direction of his horse. This gave Slocum a perfect view from above of her ample-sized breasts. He reached down and cupped them, intending to draw her upright. Again she surprised him by batting his hands away.

"No," she said firmly. "You've got to catch me."

"Do I get to brand you after I catch you?" he asked.

"Depends on how good it is when you catch me," she said, her lips darting back to his rigid stalk and lapping from the base to the sensitive, quivering tip. Then she twisted about and scuttled away on hands and knees along the shore of the pond. The auburn-haired beauty looked back over her shoulder to see what Slocum was going to do.

He shucked off his shirt and started skinning out of his jeans as she bucked and cavorted about on all fours, pretending to be a horse. Before long, Slocum had shed his useless clothing.

"My, my, what a fine sight," she said, looking at his groin. "Nothing on but . . . that." She laughed, then did a poor imitation of a whinny. The woman spun about, her white bottom flashing in the sun as she scurried off.

Slocum dropped to all fours and hurried after her, catching her at the edge of the watering hole. He reached out and grabbed her around her trim waist, pulling her back. She let out a shriek and wiggled her buttocks backward toward his crotch.

His steely length parted the creamy half moons and plunged forward. For a moment, Slocum thought he had missed his target, but she reached back between her legs, stroked lightly over his balls, then found his shaft and guided it directly to the spot they both sought to have filled.

Slocum gulped as he sank deep up her most intimate passage from behind. Warm, wet, tight—he was completely surrounded by her sheath of female flesh. Then he was crushed. She grunted, tightened her muscles and clamped down firmly on him.

The woman began thrusting her hips backward, urging him to sink even deeper into her body. Slocum didn't have to be told what she wanted—he wanted the same thing. He slipped back a few inches, then rammed forward with all his strength, crushing her firm buttocks against his tightly muscled belly. He rotated around and around, as if he were a spoon stirring about in her bowl, then he pulled back.

"Harder, harder," she begged. As he slid forward, she jammed her hips backward to meet his thrust, giving them both a teeth-rattling penetration. Slocum worked faster then and found he couldn't deliver his fleshy ramrod hard enough to satisfy her.

Reaching around her waist, he held her in position as he began stroking furiously. This worked better, since she didn't bounce away from his passionate intrusion. He moved his hand to the slash between her legs and caressed the pinkly scalloped nether lips with his fingers even as he stroked forcefully from behind.

This was the combination that sent skyrockets flaring in the young woman's trim, supple body. She quivered and shook and then let out a shriek that could have been heard all the way to Fort Bridger as passion seized her in its fierce grip.

Slocum arched his back as he tried to sink ever deeper into her, but he found the going increasingly more difficult. His control slipped away as heat from carnal friction mounted and her small diameter tightened even more to crush him. Banked fires in his loins turned into a raging conflagration that spread all the way down his length. Try as he might, he couldn't restrain himself.

He spilled his seed as she let out another soul-searing cry of release. Locked together, they rode out the last of the gusty desire blowing through their bodies.

She sank forward to the muddy ground, then lithely rolled onto her back and lifted her legs in an inviting vee.

"That's it?" she said. "No more?"

"You tuckered me out," Slocum said. "What are you doing out here all alone?"

"Afraid I might have a husband lurking in the bushes? That'd be fun, letting some guy watch while you forced yourself on me."

"I don't remember having to do much convincing," Slocum said.

"No, you're right. I had to convince you. Like I have to do again." She wiggled away, her long legs kicking up foam from the water. She immersed herself totally and got the mud off her flawless white skin.

"You didn't answer me. Who are you and why are you out here all by yourself?"

"My name's Ella, and I'm an artist. I decided this was a lovely spot to draw some landscapes. That cow wandered by and I chose to use her as a subject."

"You draw trees and cows?" Slocum splashed into the water beside her, washing off the trail dust and mud he had accumulated during their lovemaking on the bank.

"I don't like that kind of artistry as much as other forms," Ella said, moving closer. Her fingers stroked up and down Slocum's length. To his surprise, he began to harden again.

"What other forms?" he asked.

"I vastly prefer the dynamic to the still life."

The seductive auburn-haired vixen showed him how much she preferred motion to inaction. He was no artist but he had to agree.

3

"Hai-ya!" Slocum shouted, using the end of his rope to goad the heifer along. As he rode into the twilight, he reflected on what a good day it had become. He had not intended to remain in the Wyoming rangeland until Chafee made the offer for him to work as a cowboy for the Triple Cross. When he had ridden out this morning, he hadn't realized how the day would be spent so pleasurably beside a watering hole—and in it—with the heart-stoppingly exquisite Ella Weedin.

They had frolicked in the pool, then moved their amorous activities to the shade under a cottonwood. After that, their desires slaked, they had lain together talking for most of an hour. Slocum had been circumspect about revealing too much of his background, but Ella had proven open and aboveboard about her life.

She was from Boston, but unlike any other Easterner Slocum had ever encountered. The auburn-haired artist had come out West to sketch landscapes and to take the air, as she'd put it. From what Slocum could tell, there was nothing wrong with either her lungs or her chest. Most who professed a similar reason for travel had tuberculosis. She was healthy and lusty, and Slocum had found himself taking quite a liking to her.

He had looked at several sketches in her folio and had to admit they were good. They were drawings of places where he had been and that he knew well enough to note her attention to detail. The heifer he herded back to the Triple Cross had been recorded with almost photographic detail by her swift pencil strokes on canvas before he had come along and disturbed her work.

Slocum smiled. It had been quite a while since he'd felt as good about a day as he did now.

He snapped his rope and got the critter into a pen behind the barn, then dismounted and tended his Appaloosa before going to the bunkhouse.

"You finally got back," Chafee said in greeting. Three other cowboys tended their gear and didn't bother looking up. They'd never cottoned much to Slocum. He thought Chafee was the only overtly friendly one in the outfit.

"One healthy breeder returned to the fold," Slocum said.

"That's good," Chafee said. The man's tone put Slocum on edge.

"What's happened?"

"Nuthin' what ain't happened a dozen times before," grumbled another cowboy, never looking up from his chore of waxing down his saddle and bridle. "Chafee," the man said, looking up for the first time, "you go talk to Old Man Mathiesen and get my pay. I'm quittin'."

"He's not feeling too good and hasn't for a couple weeks. You know that. And you know everybody's paid on the first. You leave now, Longmeadow, and you ride out with only the money you got in your pocket."

"Ain't fair. We're not lawmen. Not right to ask us to do more."

"What's going on?" Slocum asked. He rested his hand on the ebony butt of his six-shooter.

"Rustlers," Chafee said grimly. "Rustlers are giving us fits. What they can't steal, they shoot. Dangedest thing I ever saw. Most thieves'll leave behind what they can't take, in case they can come back later and steal the cattle then. Not these owlhoots."

"They shot the cattle?" Slocum shook his head. That made no sense, although he had come across men so mean they'd shoot their own dog for the hell of it.

"The boss has lost two hundred head in the past three months. Stolen. Now the bastards are taking to shooting what they don't steal." Chafee sounded bitter, and Slocum knew the reason. With so many of the cowhands heading north to find their fortune in goldfields, the remaining men were spread thin over the expansive Triple Cross Ranch. Fewer men meant a better chance for rustling to succeed.

Slocum heaved a sigh. "You know about where the rustlers are operating?"

"You thinking on going after them?" asked Chafee. "That's foolish, Slocum. Even if all of us rode together, it'd be pure suicide. I spotted them a while back from way off and counted no fewer than ten rustlers in that gang."

"I'm a fair tracker," Slocum said, understating his abilities considerably. "If I catch sight of them, I can follow them to their hideout. The cavalry's likely to have an interest in them." Slocum knew there was a sizable garrison outside the small town centered around the saloon. The horse soldiers had fought well during the Utah War but hadn't done much since. Somehow, they never could find the time to track down rustlers or even stir much beyond the bars in Fort Bridger.

"Let me get this straight. You find their lair, then lead the soldiers there?" Chafee stroked his stubbled chin. "Naw," he said coming to a decision. "That's too dangerous. It's mighty appealing, thinking we might stop them, but it's too dangerous, no matter how good a scout you are." Chafee's eyes fixed on Slocum's.

"I'm good enough to find them and smart enough not to tangle with them, if I'm outnumbered. The only way to stop the loss is to stop the thieves."

"But they're taking to *shooting* the beeves. Don't know why."

"Might be they're mistakin' our stock for buffalos," spoke up another of the cowboys. This provoked a good-natured argument that lightened the mood considerably, but Slocum wasn't interested in such camaraderie. All through the fine dinner Mrs. Mathiesen laid out for them, he thought about where his duty to the Triple Cross lay. Stopping the loss of cattle was about at the top. If Chafee and the others weren't up for it, he was, because Mr. Mathiesen was bedridden and unable to do any of the tracking himself.

He went to sleep in the bunkhouse that night, vowing to be on the trail by sunup. He'd put a stop to the rustling or know the reason.

Slocum stood and looked around. He had almost not believed Chafee when the foreman claimed the rustlers were shooting cattle and leaving them behind, but that's what had happened. The evidence was drawing flies at Slocum's feet. A small bullet hole in the head showed where someone had used the steer for target practice.

Taking a few steps back from the coyote-gnawed carcass, Slocum began a slow circuit around the area, hunting for clues to the man who'd gunned down a helpless bovine. More than twenty minutes of careful searching finally uncovered a pair of spent cartridges. The brass gleamed in the sun as Slocum held up one and studied it.

Other than it being a .44, Slocum wasn't able to figure out much more. The rifle firing it was new, from the look of the cartridge and the way the needle-sharp firing pin imprinted. He tossed the evidence of the cattle crime away

and began a new search, this time for the boot prints of
the man who had done the shooting.

Slocum frowned when he found the trail. The man
didn't wear boots. The shoe prints weren't anything Slocum had ever seen, either. Wind and sun had dulled the
once-distinct prints but not enough to prevent Slocum
from knowing right away when he found the man wearing
them.

"Not store-bought boots, not with flimsy soles like
that," he decided. A cobbler had put these together special
for the man wearing them. Slocum began forming a pic-
ture of the outlaw killing Triple Cross cattle and leaving
them behind for the buzzards and coyotes. A rich fellow,
buying custom made shoes and a brand-new rifle. No self-
respecting cowboy would wear thin-soled shoes like the
ones he'd tracked, but someone from back East might.
From the length of stride, the man was about five-eight.

He soon found where the man had mounted and ridden
off. Slocum fetched his Appaloosa and followed the trail.
The rider had made no effort to conceal his tracks. Slocum
reckoned the man didn't know how. More information,
but he wasn't sure what to make of it.

He topped a rise and looked down on about the most
curious sight he had ever seen. A dozen men struggled
with wheelbarrows, moving rock out of a large, shallow
pit. In the middle of the pit stretched a white skeleton, but
one made from rock. Two others knelt and used small
knives and chisels to pick away at the clay surrounding
the bones.

Whoever these men were, they weren't rustlers. But the
trail led directly to this camp.

Slocum rode down the slope and received only passing
notice from the workers. They weren't dressed as he
might expect laborers to be in the warm Wyoming summer. Two wore white shirts with collars open. Hardly the

rough clothing he would have expected from men pushing wheelbarrows.

Then he spotted the well-dressed man supervising the skeleton cleaning. The portly man sweated profusely because of his fastened collar and perfectly knotted silk cravat. As he walked toward Slocum, he left distinctive footprints in the dust. He was about the right height and wore the shoes Slocum had tracked. His hair flew every which way, but his beard was neatly combed and parted in the middle, almost to his cleft chin.

Slocum had his man, and he looked like anything but a rustler.

"Good day, sir," the man called. He shielded his eyes against the sun and peered up at Slocum. "What can we do for you?"

"You own a rifle?"

"Why, of course, sir. What manner of question is that?" The man's attitude turned brusque. "You are wasting my precious time with your foolish questions."

"They're not so foolish if you've been shooting Mr. Mathiesen's cattle. That's about the same as rustling."

"What are you accusing me of, sir!" The man pulled himself up to his full height and struck a pose, a thumb thrust under one armhole of his vest, and one foot forward so he could rock back. "I am none other than Edward Drinker Cope!"

"Thanks for giving me your moniker," Slocum said. "That'll make it easier for the cavalry to arrest you." He had started to wheel his Appaloosa around when the man let out an aggrieved cry.

"Sir! Stop! We must discuss this curious matter."

"Nothing curious about it. You or one of the men in your camp," Slocum said, eyeing the others who continued to work furiously on the unearthed pile of bones, "have been shooting my boss's cattle. That's destruction of valuable property. Not a one of the Triple Cross cattle lost hasn't been branded."

"Branded? That curious marking on the hindquarter?" Cope looked confused. "I didn't realize those cattle belonged to anyone. I was told this is all open range."

"Some of it is; most belongs to Mr. Mathiesen. You shot a Triple Cross cow on Triple Cross land."

"I am ever so sorry for this confusion on my part. I had no idea it was wrong to do so. Why, I've shot buffalo from the train and no one complained."

Slocum held his tongue. Nobody but the Pawnees who depended on those buffalo would complain. He had seen more than one train passenger commit the very offense Cope admitted so freely. Slocum had no problem bagging a buffalo if his belly grumbled loud enough. The tongue was especially good eating, but to wantonly slaughter and leave the meat for the buzzards and coyotes was a waste that set his teeth on edge.

"Accept my profuse apologies. I assure you, it won't happen again."

"Mathiesen is still out his cattle. How many have you shot?" Slocum knew of one and figured there had to be more. The one he had discovered might not have been the one Chafee had found.

"Why, I cannot say. Several. Two or three."

"That few?" pressed Slocum. He saw Cope go red in the face and begin to bluster. "Might have been as many as a dozen."

"Not that many. Half that. I'll allow as to how I shot five, but I did so under the false impression those were wild creatures."

"I reckon if you stop killing Mr. Mathiesen's herd and pay for the ones you shot—you did dress them out?"

"Why, yes, no, I can't say. What do you mean?"

"You carved 'em up and ate them," Slocum said bluntly.

"One or two. The others were convenient targets. I knew they weren't bison, but could have been. From a distance, it is difficult to tell."

Slocum considered how easy it would be to put this fool out of his misery, but if he laid him out, Mathiesen would never get his due for the dead beeves.

"Yes, I shall pay. Top dollar, to show my contrition."

"Two hundred dollars it is, then," Slocum said. The rest of Cope's crew bent over their work, snickering. They knew their leader had been caught slaughtering cattle. Slocum had no truck with any of the workmen. If they knew Cope was killing the cattle and hadn't stopped his wanton ways, they were as guilty as he was.

"Forty dollars apiece! That's robbery!" cried Cope.

"Ten cows, twenty dollars each."

"I only killed five. The rest were shot by that black-guard Marsh!"

Cope looked more closely at Slocum, as if suspecting him of some duplicity.

"You don't work for Marsh, do you? No, you're the man Sanborn approached at the fort. You turned him down. Leigh told me."

"Leigh?" Slocum remembered the Eastern dude whose fancy clothes had seen better days, and the brief conversation outside the Fort Bridger saloon. "He your foreman?"

"Yes, of course, he is."

"Why do you and Marsh shoot it out? Over a pile of bones?" Slocum looked curiously at the huge bleached skeleton embedded in rock that the crew worked to free.

"He is a scoundrel and a liar. He is guilty of buying his best specimens rather than finding them himself. He is—"

"I don't much care what bad blood there is between the two of you," Slocum interrupted. "You said Marsh shot some of Mr. Mathiesen's stock, too?"

"If there are ten dead cows, then he shot as many as I!"

Curiously, this admission of guilt appeared to be a matter of pride with Cope. Even in something as low-down as cattle shooting, he wasn't going to be outdone by his rival.

"Where's Leigh?" Slocum asked, looking around the dig site.

"He's out . . . scouting." The evasive answer told Slocum that Cope's foreman was up to no good. "We can use an experienced frontiersman such as yourself, sir," Cope gushed on. "Would you agree to hire onto my expedition?"

"To look for bones?" asked Slocum. This was as harebrained an idea as any he'd ever heard.

"Yes! To advance the science of—"

"Paleontology," Slocum said, finishing the professor's sentence. "Leigh already made his pitch. No, thanks. I'm happy working for the Triple Cross."

"If you should decide to leave that worthy, please come here first in your quest for future employment. Don't let that scoundrel Marsh hire you. You'd rue the day!"

Slocum waited impatiently while Cope wrote out a check drawn on an Eastern bank in the sum of one hundred dollars. He wasn't sure how good it would be, but it gave Mathiesen some small recompense for his slaughtered cattle if the bank at Fort Bridger accepted it and exchanged a short stack of double eagles for it.

If it didn't, Mathiesen was within his right to come and collect—or have his cowboys do it for him since he was so sickly. From the loyalty Chafee showed his boss, Slocum figured Cope would pony up the money in a split second if the check didn't clear the bank.

"You are going to confront that ruffian Marsh?" asked Cope.

"The Triple Cross can't afford to lose any more cattle,"

Slocum said, swinging into the saddle. The entire dig took on an air of unreality to him. The men struggling to chip away bits from around the skeleton might as well have been wherever they came from back East for all the support they gave their boss. They made a point of averting their eyes and trying not to eavesdrop, but Slocum knew they were taking in every word of his discussion with Cope.

"You make that miscreant pay!" shouted Cope as Slocum turned to ride away. He fancied himself a judge of men. Any number of poker games had shown Slocum he was more often right about men than wrong, but he couldn't figure out Edward Cope.

He rode in the direction the paleontologist had pointed, wondering how long he would be in the saddle. It took the better part of what remained of the day to reach a site that Slocum might have mistaken for Cope's, had it not been for the twenty grueling miles he had ridden. This skeleton was stretched out, partly embedded in the rock. A half dozen men scurried about, chipping and scraping, doing things Slocum could only guess at. The only difference between these men and the ones back in Cope's camp lay in the way they were dressed.

Slocum felt more at home among men in buckskins and canvas and wearing decent boots.

He watched the activity in the camp around this new skeleton until he was sure they had seen him. Only then did Slocum ride slowly toward the camp. He hadn't missed the sentries posted in the rocks above the bones being unearthed, or the rifles in those men's hands. From their look, Slocum guessed they were hard-bitten men used to firearms—and killing.

As he drew closer to the skeleton, he saw this was different from the one Cope worked to unbury. The man who had approached him first at Fort Bridger came forth from a tent pitched a few yards away.

Sanborn had been his name. The man with him was probably Othniel Marsh, but Slocum wasn't looking at them. He stared at the third figure emerging from the tent.

Ella Weedin.

4

"I hadn't expected to see you again, Mr. Slocum," Ella said, grinning her infectious grin.

"You know this cowboy?" asked the one Slocum had pegged as Marsh.

"Of course, I do, Othniel," she said, her smile turning just a tad wicked. That made Slocum uneasy wondering if the leader of this bone hunting expedition had a claim to her. If so, it made his business here all the more complicated.

"You're Professor Marsh?" Slocum asked, wanting to get to the heart of the matter. From the time he had spent with Ella, he knew she was not likely to let sleeping dogs lie. She would stir and poke and agitate until the pot boiled.

"I am."

"He's the cowboy I tried to hire in town, sir," spoke up Sanborn. The tattered-looking foreman looked from Slocum to Ella. The questions were written all over his face, but he didn't voice them. "I suspect he has come to his senses and come to join us. Isn't that so?"

"Not exactly," Slocum said. He found it impossible to look at either Marsh or Sanborn. His eyes fixed on Ella.

She noticed and pulled her shoulders back a mite, forcing her breasts hard against the already tight fabric of her blouse. If she took in much of a breath, Slocum was sure her buttons would pop.

He shook himself free of her sexy spell to concentrate on business.

"I rode here straight from Cope's camp."

"Cope! That ignoramus!" flared Othniel Marsh. The professor ran his hands through his thinning, combed-back hair and got a wild look in his eyes. He was so mad his mustachioed upper lip quivered like it had the palsy. "I'll have his guts for garters!"

"I collected money from him because he'd been shooting my boss's cattle. I'm working for Mathiesen, the owner of the Triple Cross." Slocum found himself wanting to explain more so he wouldn't have to later. He was certain Ella would begin furnishing all kinds of details he had given her, causing both men to wonder how she had come by the information.

"He's a danger to everyone out here," declared Marsh. "A danger and a complete imbecile. A dolt. A . . . a . . ." He began sputtering when he couldn't think of any further names to call his rival.

"Cope said you've been doing a little poaching yourself. Have you shot and butchered any Triple Cross cattle?" This time Slocum fixed his gaze on the foreman. If Sanborn reacted, he'd know Cope had been right about both parties being responsible. The sudden jerk, as if Sanborn had been stuck by a needle, told Slocum he had found another source of sudden death for Mr. Mathiesen's beeves.

"We might have found one or two strays," Sanborn said. "We didn't know they belonged to anyone."

"Figured they got those brands on their rumps all natural-like? Maybe they all were struck by lightning in the same way?" Slocum asked sarcastically. "Ten have been shot. Cope's paid for five. Don't see any reason it wouldn't be the right thing for you to pay for the other five."

"We only shot one!" blazed Marsh. Then he quieted a bit and added, "Well, perhaps it was more." He looked to Sanborn for support.

His foreman said, "Five? Too many. Not more than four."

"Twenty-five a head," Slocum said, inflating the price per cow since he wasn't inclined to dicker over the actual number of cattle shot. "That's a hundred dollars you owe Mr. Mathiesen."

"Make out a check, Othniel," Ella said, her smile creeping ever larger. "I'm sure it will be delivered to the proper hands. Mr. Slocum is an honest, honorable man."

"I am, ma'am," he said.

"I'll make out a bank draft to this Mathiesen fellow," Marsh said. He went back into his tent, grumbling as he went about rising costs for the expedition. Sanborn cast a quick look at Slocum, then at Ella, before following his boss.

"I had thought we would be like the proverbial ships passing in the night," the auburn-haired woman said. Her bright blue eyes took on an inner light in the dying of the day. "I'm glad it wasn't like that."

"You said you were an artist. You never mentioned working for the professor," Slocum said. He dismounted and stood awkwardly, looking from Ella to the tent. It wouldn't have surprised him unduly to see a rifle pointing out from between the tent flaps, although he doubted either Sanborn or Marsh was likely to drygulch him. They'd leave that to the hard cases in the rocks above the dig.

"Oh, I am. You certainly said I showed great ability when we were—"

"Why dig up old bones?" Slocum cut in, not wanting to get the provocative woman started.

"You might say I have a great interest in bones," she said, moving a little closer. Only when she saw how uncomfortable he was did she back away. "I sketch the skeletons for Professor Marsh. He had brought along a photographer to take pictures, but Cope hired him away."

"I didn't see any sign Cope was having photographs taken," Slocum said.

"Of course not. A shame how the photographer's plates were all accidentally exposed. Ruined by light. He had to send back to St. Louis for more, and that is taking a very long time."

Slocum wondered what role Ella had in this sabotage, but he didn't ask. She might tell him.

"You said you were from Boston," Slocum said.

"I am. I happened to drift westward to St. Louis to complete my masterwork, a pictorial study of America from coast to coast."

"So Marsh hired you in St. Louis?"

"I was riding the train out here, just after he had discovered he no longer had a photographer in his employ. My being from Boston did not prejudice him in hiring me."

"Why should it?" Slocum frowned.

"I come from across the Charles River, near Harvard. The professor is from Yale." She rushed on with her explanation when it was obvious he didn't understand. "Think of it as a rivalry, a feud between brothers. But blood is never spilled, except in an academic sense."

"Cope and Marsh could settle their differences with a good fistfight," Slocum said.

"It goes deeper than one whaling the tar out of the other," Ella said with some gusto, as if she relished their animosity. "But you're beginning to understand their sense of competition. One finding a new dinosaur before the other would be ever so much more satisfying than punching the other. Trumping the other's discovery with a new one or pointing out the errors in a published research paper or a skeletal reconstruction on display in a museum would be even better."

"Like an Indian counting coup," Slocum said.

"If I understand the concept properly, yes," she said. "You do amaze me, John. Not only are you good-looking in a rugged, weather-beaten way, you are smart—and most expert at certain intimate pursuits."

"Here," called Marsh, returning from the tent. He waved a length of green paper in the air to dry the ink. "This should settle accounts in full."

"It will, if none of your men go around shooting Mr. Mathiesen's cattle again," Slocum said.

"Let me show Mr. Slocum around, Othniel," Ella cut in. "I'm certain he would find it amusing. Perhaps he might even decide to join our ranks when he sees how expert your dig is."

From Sanborn's frown, Slocum guessed that the foreman was more than a little interested in Ella himself. Who knew? Perhaps they had enjoyed a tryst by some other watering hole, and Sanborn considered her his property. Ella struck Slocum as the kind of woman who acted on a whim and didn't understand when men around her got all riled.

"Do so. You would be a most welcome addition to our expedition, Mr. Slocum," Marsh said. He took Sanborn by the arm and guided the foreman away, toward the skeleton being unearthed inch by inch. From the way Sanborn resisted, Slocum knew the foreman did have a letch for Ella, not that he could be blamed for that.

"These are the partial remains of a new type of dinosaur," Ella said, locking her arm through his and steering him in the direction exactly opposite to that taken by Marsh and Sanborn. "The first indication is that there were large bony plates on the back, much like a sailfish."

"Don't know about sailfish," Slocum said, "but I've

seen some lizards with a wide collar around their necks. They fan it out when they're in the sun."

"For heating or cooling, yes," Ella said. "You are most observant, John. I think you would make a splendid addition to the professor's technical staff."

"Them?" He looked at the workers painstakingly removing rock and clay from around the skeletal remains. "I don't know why they're even doing that."

"To free the entire skeleton from the rock, of course."

"But you said it's not complete. Not like the one I saw a ways off."

Ella stopped dead in her tracks and turned. Her blue eyes bored into his green ones.

"You saw another skeleton that looked like this one?"

"Only more complete," Slocum said. "Riding here from Cope's camp, I passed a broad, level field and thought it was peculiar how these skeletons were turning up all over the place when all I'd noticed before on the prairie were buffalo carcasses bleaching in the sun." Now he saw pieces of bone poking out of rock layers everywhere he turned. Slocum realized that a man only saw what he wanted.

"Show me. I want you to show me!"

"It's getting dark," Slocum said. "It's not safe to be out now."

"Not safe? What were you going to do to me?" she asked coyly.

"Not me. There are Pawnee, Shawnee and Arapaho on the prowl."

"I didn't think Indians went out after sundown. Some silly superstition of theirs."

"You're thinking of the Apaches. They're deathly afraid of rattlesnakes. Other tribes, the ones around here, don't have any taboo against raiding in the dark."

"You've still got to show me. We have to claim it before Cope!"

Slocum saw that the fever of discovery ran as high in Ella as it did in her employer.

"Please, John, this is an important find, if it's as complete you say. I'm not doubting you, but paleontology is a complex and demanding science."

"I saw what I saw," Slocum said, eyeing the shadows cloaking Marsh's nearby discovery and comparing what was there with what he had seen. They matched, only his was whole.

"Take me. Now!"

"Right here? You are a frisky filly," he said, taking a little revenge on her for making him uneasy in front of Marsh and Sanborn earlier. For a moment, Ella looked startled. Then she laughed.

"You are quite a card, John. The more I'm with you, the more I like you. Now show me this fabulous pile of bones. Perhaps you can show me yours later." The wicked, taunting grin flickered across her lips, but Slocum saw she cared less about him than she did about the skeleton.

By the time Slocum got to his horse, she had saddled another and was ready to ride. He wasn't certain what she'd told Marsh, but the professor looked indifferent to her leaving with a stranger. Sanborn, though, looked mad enough to chew nails and spit out tacks.

"Where are you going?" he demanded angrily.

"We'll be back before you know it," Ella said airily. She put her heels to her horse's flanks and rocketed off. Slocum followed at a more sedate pace since it was too dark to hurry. The woman might not care if her horse stepped in a prairie dog hole and broke its leg, but he had become fond of his Appaloosa and intended riding the mottled stallion for a long, long time.

"Which way, John?" Ella called.

"Not that way," he said, looking up into the darkening sky to get a fix on the evening star and the constellations slowly wheeling into view. He cut off at an angle, letting her catch up with him.

"You're mad at me," she said. "Don't be. This is important."

"To you or to Marsh?"

"Both of us. Drawing the dinosaurs he finds will make me famous. The pictures will be seen throughout the world, and I might get more work than I can handle."

"And Marsh would think your drawings had made him famous, so he'd be beholden to you," Slocum said. To his surprise, she laughed harshly.

"You don't know him, John. He would *never* think I had helped him. Always the other way. His conceit knows no bounds."

"He and Cope sound like they're cut from the same cloth."

"There's one big difference," Ella said. "Marsh is a true academic, an expert who knows and loves his work. Cope is a poseur seeking only fame."

They rode, Ella giving a steady appraisal of the two men's failings and strengths. Slocum hardly listened. He had already come to the same conclusion based on only fleeting contact with both men. Now and then he glanced at the sky to get his bearings, but mostly he watched Ella as she bounced along on the horse. His thoughts returned to their pleasurable afternoon dalliance and wondered if it would happen again. At first, he had thought she wanted another roll in the hay, but her eagerness to see the bone field he had found changed his mind.

She was as driven to uncover new dinosaur bones as either Othniel Marsh or Edward Cope.

"There," Slocum said, reining in. "That's the spot."

"I need to see it myself. Are there bones poking out of the ground? That might not be good. The wind and rain wear them down eventually and ruin their assembly into a whole creature."

Slocum dismounted and led his horse forward to the spot he had found on his way to Marsh's camp. He stumbled in the dark. Looking down he saw a rock poking up from the ground.

"John, be careful!" she called. "That's a rib you almost broke!"

For a moment he thought she meant his rib. Then he got a better look at what he had thought was a rock. A cylindrical protrusion might have been part of some giant creature's rib cage. But the size would have been immense.

"I've seen elephants," Slocum said, "but this can't be part of one. It'd mean something three or four times as big." His eyes worked along the arch of what Ella had deemed a rib.

"We need to light a bonfire, John. Or a torch. Can you make a torch so I can investigate? This looks like a major discovery. A big one that'll bring a glint even to Marsh's eyes. And he thought he was jaded," she said, chuckling. "Just wait until he lays eyes on this!"

Slocum scouted the area for dried limbs or anything else that might make a torch. As he walked, a curious feeling settled into the pit of his stomach. He had the feeling of being watched. Standing stock still, he listened hard but heard nothing. Even the restless wind had died for the moment, making it so quiet Slocum could hear his hair grow.

He picked up a fallen branch from a pine tree and used his knife to cut small slivers off it, leaving it partly peeled. The slivers would burn for a spell.

Long enough for Ella to see what stretched out across the field.

Slocum walked slowly back to where the woman crawled on hands and knees, her face pressed down close to the ground so she could examine the bone jutting up.

He stopped again and listened once more. Their horses

nickered and Ella's breath came shallow and fast from her excitement. But there wasn't another sound. Nothing.

"Light it, John. I need to see," she said.

Slocum fumbled out the tin with his lucifers, hesitated and then set fire to the fuzz stick he had whittled. The shavings blazed brightly, casting an eerie light across the entire field.

"No sound," Slocum said. "There's nothing moving."

He threw the torch in one direction and dived in the other, arms wrapping around the woman and forcing her flat onto the ground.

"John, really. There'll be time later. I—"

Slocum's instincts had been right. The rest of Ella's complaint was swallowed by the sharp crack of a rifle bullet and the slug's whine as it glanced off the top of the petrified bone she had been examining.

5

"Who's shooting at me?" cried Ella Weedin. She struggled in Slocum's arms, but he refused to let her up. They were sitting ducks out in the middle of the level landscape. "Let me *go!*"

She kicked Slocum and wrenched free with a powerful surge. As he had thought, she presented a better target for the bushwhacker skulking out in the dark. Slocum saw Ella recoil when the hair on top of her head puffed up a little. A bullet had missed killing her by the merest fraction of an inch.

"Stay down," he ordered, shoving her hard onto her back.

"This position might be more interesting if someone wasn't trying to kill us," she said. A lascivious grin flickered on her lips and then disappeared. "Who's shooting at me? Is it Cope? Othniel is not going to like this."

"We're not going to like it if we don't find better cover," Slocum said. He scanned the area at the edge of a stand of pines almost fifty yards away. If the bushwhacker hid there, he was one hell of a marksman. Even as Slocum thought their attacker was somewhere closer, he saw the foot-long tongue of orange flash from a rifle muzzle. This shot produced a sorrowful sound, then Ella's horse keeled over, kicked once and lay still.

"They shot my horse!" She was even more incensed at this than she was that the bushwhacker intended to ventilate her flawless white hide.

"Get to the horse," Slocum snapped. Although she protested, he grabbed her arm and dragged her in the direction of the dead animal. He shoved her down behind the mountain of dead flesh and said, "Stay here."

"I can't use the horse as a shield, John. That's not right."

He stared at her, wondering if everyone from the other side of the Mississippi was plumb crazy.

"It'll keep you alive. Think of it this way. The horse gave its life so you could keep on kicking."

He didn't wait to see if this logic worked with the woman. He feinted up, drew fire with his hat, then rolled to his feet and sprinted for his Appaloosa. The horse pawed the ground nervously but stood its ground in spite of the ruckus. This wasn't the first time it had been at the edge of a gunfight. With a kiss from Lady Luck, it wouldn't be the last, either.

Slocum vaulted into the saddle, stayed low and rode at a gallop straight for the cluster of trees. As he neared the pines, he drew his six-shooter and got ready to fire. His horse blasted past the point where he had spotted the rifleman and then thundered blindly through the forest. Low branches slashed at Slocum's face, making it hard to see. But he didn't slow his attack. If he had, he would have provided a decent target.

Bursting into a grassy clearing turned to liquid silver by the rising moon, Slocum wheeled his horse around and looked at his backtrail, expecting to see someone pop out to take a shot at him.

Silence. The same silence as before. Slocum felt the hair on the back of his neck ripple. This eerie quiet should have alerted him before. Small animals ought to have been making tiny sounds as they scurried about their business of feeding and breeding. Owls hunting mice and snakes. Other nocturnal birds flapping about. Wolves and coyotes slinking away from humans. Something.

Silence.

Slocum knew that meant something—someone—had disturbed them enough so they went to ground. He gripped his six-gun and waited for any betraying sound, but there wasn't any. Slocum sucked in his breath, then let it out slowly. No white man crept about in the forest this quietly, except an Indian-trained mountain man. Some of those skilled frontiersmen might call Fort Bridger their home, but Slocum thought it was more likely that he faced an Indian. Chafee had warned him of the Arapahos being active in the area.

Cocking his head to the side let him hear the sound of distant horses. He couldn't tell for sure but it sounded like a half dozen or more ponies. He didn't face a single brave out to win himself a scalp. There might be an entire hunting party moving through the woods around him.

At least, he hoped it was a hunting party. He and Ella had a chance to get away if all the Indians wanted to do was bag a deer or two to feed their families. If this was a war party, they wouldn't rest until Slocum was dead and Ella was their slave.

Slocum holstered his six-shooter and drew the Winchester from its saddle sheath. He needed something more powerful to defend himself as he slowly rode in the direction of the horses he had heard. Not levering a round into the chamber prevented quick response, but it also allowed him to make a ghostlike approach. Guiding his Appaloosa using only his knees, Slocum lifted the rifle to his shoulder when he saw shadows moving across shadows.

He hesitated for a moment, then saw three new shad-

ows. Quickly cocking the rifle produced a sound that echoed through the still forest like an explosion. He brought
the rifle to bear and fired in one smooth motion, then
began firing methodically. Outnumbered as he was, he
had to draw blood to put the fear into the Indians. If he
missed and they had a chance to circle him, he was a
goner.

Slocum took scant pleasure in the anguished cry of a
brave. He turned slightly in the saddle and kept firing until
the magazine came up empty. With a bone-chilling cry,
he drew his Colt Navy and charged. Slocum wasn't sure
if the Indians were ahead lying in wait or if they had
slipped away into the night. Venting a bloodcurdling rebel
yell, he plunged through the undergrowth and fired left
and right.

When his six-gun came up empty, he turned and headed
back toward the spot where he had left Ella.

"John!" she called, standing and waving foolishly. "Are
you all right?"

"Stay down!" he shouted. He bent low and got as much
speed from his tiring horse as he could. Every inch of the
way he expected a bullet to slash through his back, but
he reached the woman, hunched down as he rode past and
caught her. The sudden weight as his arm encircled her
almost jerked him from the saddle, but he held on and
rode.

With a savage yank, he got Ella off the ground and
deposited behind him. She clung to him for dear life.

"John," she gasped out. "D-did you kill whoever was
shooting at us?"

"Indians," he said. "Arapaho, probably." The Appaloosa began to falter, forcing Slocum to let the horse pick
a slower gait. Carrying almost twice the usual weight, the
horse could not keep up the frantic gallop without dying
under Slocum.

As he slowed, Slocum looked around to be sure he

wasn't blundering into a trap. His mouth went dry when he saw crossed lances thrust into the ground. He had missed them before, but their presence explained a great deal.

"This is an Indian burial ground," he said. "Sacred earth."

"Is that what those spears mean?" Ella asked. "I saw another pair at the edge of the field while I was waiting for you to come back for me." She snuggled closer, her arms circling his waist intimately. She laid her cheek against his shoulder, so he could feel her warm breath gusting in and out. "I knew you'd come back."

"I couldn't leave you," Slocum said. His mind raced. The Indians were protecting the spot where they conducted their burial rituals. He hadn't seen any remnants of the elevated funeral pyres they used, but he had not looked, either.

"Marsh is going to be so happy. It's a new dinosaur," Ella said.

"We can't go back there. It's desecration."

"Oh, bother," she said, her lips close to his ear now. "Dead's dead. Isn't that what paleontology is all about? Dead things. Bones?"

"Those are human bones back there."

"Not the fossil you found. The one at the main dig has a sail along its back, but this one had three horns on its head. Othniel will know if it is a new species. Of course, it might be from a species already found, but it would take his expertise to determine that."

"You're not listening," Slocum said. "That's a cemetery. A burial ground. It's sacred to the Arapaho."

"Oh, the professor will sweet talk them into letting him look for dinosaur skeletons. He's not going to disinter any of their dead. He wants old bones. *Ancient* bones."

"They don't know or care about that," Slocum said. He

looked over his shoulder, fearing that the Arapaho were coming after him for such blasphemy.

"You're not frightened of ghosts, are you, John? Goodness gracious!" Ella laughed in delight. "A big, strong, *virile* man like you, afraid of spooks."

"That wasn't any ghost shooting at us. It was a living, breathing Indian who was pissed that we were poking around among his dead ancestors."

"You worry too much."

Slocum said nothing. He thought Ella didn't worry enough. She hadn't learned anything from their excursion except the location of the dinosaur bones. He kept the Appaloosa moving as he reloaded his rifle and then worked on his Colt Navy. Having both weapons fully loaded again made him feel a mite better, but not much.

He felt even worse when they rode back into Marsh's camp. The sentries had spotted them a quarter mile off and had alerted Sanborn. Marsh's threadbare foreman stood with arms crossed belligerently and glaring at them.

"You took your fine time," he said crossly.

"I have to talk to Othniel," Ella said, sliding off the horse and landing lightly. "It's a major find. It's something entirely new."

"The professor will be the judge of that," Sanborn said. He glowered at Slocum. "You shouldn't be out gallivanting around after dark. This is a dangerous place."

Slocum dismounted and stretched. Every bone in his body ached, he hadn't eaten since Hector was a pup, and he was in no mood to listen to Sanborn whining.

"Don't try to dig up that fossil," Slocum said. "It's in the middle of an Arapaho burial ground."

Before Sanborn could retort, Marsh and Ella came from his tent. The professor was positively bubbling with excitement.

"That's what Ella said. All the better. They wouldn't be too inclined to move any bones they found. This might be a major breakthrough. I found part of a skull with three horns on a prior expedition but not a complete skeleton. A triceratops, that's what I'll call it. Yes."

"You'd better powwow with the Indians before you set up another camp," Slocum warned. "You might find there's not enough firepower to barge in without their medicine man's approval."

"I do love the primitives and their quaint notions," Marsh said. "Does Cope have an inkling of this spot?"

"What? No, you're the only one I've told." Slocum was confused by the sudden turn in the conversation.

"Good! I'll swoop down and recover the skeleton before that nincompoop knows!"

Marsh and Sanborn went off, discussing how best to exploit this new find. Ella hugged Slocum tightly.

"You've made him a very happy man, John." She looked up with her luminous blue eyes. "I'd like to make you a very happy man, too. But in a more intimate way." Her lips parted slightly as her tongue peeked forth.

Slocum pushed her back. He was too furious at her for anything such as she suggested.

"I've got to get back to the Triple Cross. The foreman probably thinks the rustlers have left me for coyote food."

"You don't want to—" Ella frowned. "I see. You may be right. This isn't the time or place."

"No, it isn't."

"Wait, John," she said as he started to leave. "Your horse is exhausted. Give it until morning to rest up. We can give you a meal and you can ride into town with a wagonload of fossils."

"What do they do with the bones in Fort Bridger?" he asked, curious in spite of himself. He had no intention of riding along with the wagon to find out.

"They're shipped back to New Haven in marked, numbered crates. When Professor Marsh returns to Yale University, he will assemble the skeletons and put them on display in the Peabody Museum. It is quite the place, you know."

Slocum decided it wasn't a bad idea to grab some shut-eye. Alone. He saw Sanborn holding the tent flap open a fraction of an inch so he could spy on Slocum and Ella.

"My horse can use the rest," Slocum said.

"Till cock's crow," Ella said, giving him one of her mischievous looks. She did a saucy little pirouette and walked away, just enough hitch in her hindquarters to cause a stirring to begin in Slocum. He shook himself to get rid of the feelings building like floodwater behind a dam. This was not the time or place.

From the way Sanborn watched him like a hawk, there might not be another time or place. Slocum had to wonder if only Sanborn was infatuated with the artist or if there was a more mutual attraction. Ella had shown herself to be open and not the least bit shy when it came to expressing her desires. As much as she and the professor shared their lunatic enthusiasm for finding new dinosaur remains, he could not see them also sharing a bed.

Slocum led his horse to one side of the bone field and found a rock outcropping that would serve as a partial roof over his head. He brushed down his horse, staked the Appaloosa so it could find some tender grass to eat, then spread out his bedroll to grab some sleep. Before he knew it, he heard the rattle of wagon wheels. He rolled over and squinted at the sunlight slanting down from across the broad eastern prairie lands. It was later than he usually slept, but he had been as tired as his horse.

The wagon, laden with the product of Marsh's searching for bones, rattled out of the camp. A single guard rode beside the driver. Slocum lay back and closed his eyes, thinking about the need for an armed guard on a wagon filled with soup bones. The muzzy, warm feeling slipped over him and he slept again for almost an hour.

He came awake in a rush, hand going for his Colt, when

he heard shouts in Marsh's camp. Slocum saw Ella emerge from her tent, struggling into her clothing. She went to where Sanborn and Marsh stood close together talking in low voices. Something was seriously wrong. Slocum pulled on his boots, settled his gunbelt around his waist and went to see what the fuss was all about.

"John!" she called. "It's terrible!"

"What's that?" he asked, a sinking feeling holding the pit of his stomach.

"It's good you didn't ride with them. The fossils the professor sent to Fort Bridger. Both the driver and the guard were killed!"

"How do you know?" he asked.

"Porky, here, he was riding back from Fort Bridger. He'd been locked up for drunkenness," Sanborn said, scowling at such flaunting of the law. "He saw the wagon being attacked not ten miles down the road."

"Who was it?" Slocum asked, fearing the Arapahos were exacting their revenge for treading on their sacred burial ground. He wasn't prepared for Marsh's answer.

The professor pulled himself up to his full height. It looked as if a storm cloud settled on his face. Lip quivering with emotion, Othniel Marsh said, "It was Cope. The man will stop at nothing to discredit me."

"Are you sure?" Slocum asked, more of the harried worker than Marsh. But the professor answered.

"Cope has stolen the dinosaur skeletons and will claim them as his own discovery! He is a scoundrel!" Marsh declared.

Slocum looked from Sanborn to the worker to Ella and then back to Othniel Marsh. He couldn't figure out the truth, other than that the wagon had been hijacked.

6

"Porky?" Slocum looked at Othniel Marsh's worker and wondered how he had come by the name. The man was as thin as a rail, and if he turned sideways he might disappear entirely.

"Yeah?" The man's eyes looked glazed, as if he had stopped by the saloon on his way back from Fort Bridger and his night in the calaboose for whooping it up a bit too much.

"Tell me what happened," demanded Sanborn, grabbing Porky's arms and spinning him around so he could stare into his ugly face. "Everything, man. There was a full ton of unique bones in that wagon. We can't afford to lose them. The work can't go for naught."

Slocum wondered how much of Sanborn's pretty speech was for Marsh's benefit. Or Ella's.

"The knowledge lost," moaned Marsh. "It can't fall into that knave's possession. Cope would not understand how to put the skeletons together properly. He'd put a mesohippus cranium on an archaeotherium body! He's a disgrace as a researcher and a complete reprobate morally!"

"Those are little horses and giant pigs," Ella said softly. She moved closer so she could speak to Slocum in a low voice. "These are very important finds, John. Their loss is beyond price." She looked up at him, blue eyes shining. He knew what she wanted, and he didn't want any part of it, no matter what enticing reward she might offer.

"Get everyone together!" shouted Marsh. "Arm everyone. We'll ride into Cope's camp and take back our fossils!"

"Hold on," Slocum said. He felt himself being sucked into this fight, like a leaf swirling around in a millrace. "You and Cope have shot it out before." He knew this all too well, having been caught in the middle of their wild attack as he rode into Fort Bridger. "Did it solve anything?"

"Well, no, it didn't, but only because we didn't kill him," Marsh said with startling honesty.

Slocum considered what the southwestern corner of Wyoming would be like if the hotheaded scientists took to shooting anything that moved. The Triple Cross cattle wouldn't be safe, Mathiesen's cowhands wouldn't be safe riding the range, and even worse, if either Cope or Marsh accidently shot an Arapaho, there would be a new Indian war raging before the end of the week.

"Let me do some scouting," Slocum said. "If I can't get the wagon and your bones back, at the very least I'll be able to lead the cavalry to recover everything."

"No!" cried Sanborn, obviously seeing this as a feather in Slocum's cap if he succeeded—and the resulting loss of respect for the foreman from Ella Weedin.

"Yes," countered Marsh. "I know you were a stouthearted man when I set eyes on you, Mr. Slocum. What do you want us to do? We'll ride to protect your back."

"Keep on digging here," Slocum said, not wanting Marsh either to come along and stir up an already boiling pot or to explore the bone field in the middle of the sacred Arapaho burial ground. "I'll get the wagon back."

"We're almost done here," Marsh said, frowning. "That

new spot, the one you showed Miss Weedin, we can go there and begin to—"

"Here," Slocum said sharply. "You need to stay here so I can easily find you."

Slocum silenced Sanborn's protest with a glare. He felt Ella's hand on his arm, warm and inviting, encouraging him. He wondered if Sanborn had ever had a chance with her. From the way the man acted so pompously, he doubted it. Sanborn might be a clever researcher and the more famous Marsh's right-hand man, but he wasn't the sort who appealed to Ella except as a lark.

"Hurry, John. We'll be waiting for you here," Ella said.

For a moment, Slocum thought she was going to kiss him. He didn't know what her reputation was like among the expedition, but such a public display would have branded her as a loose woman and robbed Slocum of what little authority he had. For both their sakes, she backed away and graced him with only her devilish smile.

He hurriedly saddled his Appaloosa and checked his weapons. After making certain he had a shell chambered in his Winchester, he rummaged through his saddlebags hunting for spare ammo. He had two boxes. Enough for a real fight.

Slocum swung into the saddle and looked down at the tight knot of researchers. Sanborn and Marsh argued, with Ella trying to mediate. He doubted this was a role she accepted willingly, so he could only trust that she was doing what was necessary.

He rode a few yards, then reined in and looked down on Porky. The man held a plate of beans and had finished most of it off. He cast covetous eyes toward the steaming pot where more cooked. Slocum had discovered the source of this skinny galoot's moniker. Porky could eat all day and still want another helping.

"Ten miles down the road?" Slocum asked. Porky nodded, never slowing as he spooned beans into his mouth.

Slocum's bell grumbled, since he had skipped breakfast, but he turned his Appaloosa toward the road running to Fort Bridger and headed out. The horse kept up a steady canter it could maintain for an hour or so before tiring. Slocum changed gait occasionally to give the horse a chance to rest. He had no idea what he was going to find. If Edward Cope had been responsible for the wagon theft, Slocum doubted there would be much trouble. Neither Cope nor Marsh was much when it came to shootouts. But the Arapahos might be a different matter—and there was one other player in the game Slocum had to consider. Chafee complained bitterly about rustlers stealing the Triple Cross cattle. Slocum had not run afoul of them, but that didn't mean a gang of cattle thieves wasn't ranging far and wide across this part of Wyoming.

A heavily loaded wagon filled with bones from animals dead for who knew how long wouldn't appeal to rustlers intent on stealing supplies and ammunition. If they had committed the robbery, they'd have abandoned the wagon quickly.

Slocum worked over the problems and finally decided it did no good planning for the time when he found the wagon. There was too much he didn't know. The possibility existed that the driver and guard had simply gotten fed up and driven off. Or maybe they were selling out to Cope.

Slocum just didn't know.

But he would.

He found the spot where a half dozen riders waited with their horses before he got to the part of the road where they had attacked the wagon. Slocum wiped sweat off his forehead when he found evidence that there had been quite a fight. Spent brass rifle cartridges littered the ground, shiny and bright in the noonday sun. From the pattern of where the brass hand landed, Slocum reconstructed the fight.

The wagon guard must have put up a fierce fight to save the bones—or himself. Slocum followed the wagon tracks and drew rein. He swallowed hard when he saw two bodies laying face down in a shallow ravine. One man's shirt looked familiar. Slocum recollected one of Marsh's workers having a flannel shirt with such a red-and-black checked pattern. It had struck him that it looked more like a lumberjack's shirt than that of a man toiling in the hot Wyoming sun over a stack of brittle old bones. The other dead body, riddled with lead, had to be the guard. Slocum had been right about the fight the guard had mounted against the road agents.

It had meant his death.

"Dead because of a passel of old bones," Slocum muttered. He realized he had reached for his six-shooter and hadn't noticed. Relaxing, he stood in the stirrups and tried to get a better view of the terrain stretching toward the mountains to the west. The land became rolling hills in a hurry, blocking his view. Slocum listened hard but heard only the sounds he expected on a grassland.

Walking his horse along the ruts left by the wagon quickly brought him to the summit of a low rise. He took no pleasure in spotting the wagon at the bottom of the hill. Two men lounged in the shade cast by the heavy wagon, one smoking and the other apparently taking a siesta.

Slocum drew his rifle and pulled back the hammer. The small metallic click was swallowed by distance. Even when he started down the hill, the two men didn't take note.

"Up with your hands," Slocum called, sighting along the rifle barrel at the man finishing his cigarette. The man jumped as if he had stepped on a rattler.

"Who're you?" the man sputtered. This woke up his partner, who went for his six-gun.

Slocum fired. His round ripped through the man's forearm, but it also caused the Appaloosa to rear. This gave the two thieves the chance to hightail it.

The one who had been smoking got his hogleg out and flung lead in Slocum's direction, further spooking the Appaloosa. His partner clumsily switched his six-gun to his good hand and fired, adding to the lead singing through the air.

Rather than trust that the men were more interested in escaping, Slocum slid from the saddle and hit the ground hard. He knelt and fired in the direction of the two outlaws, but they had gained their saddles and were galloping away. His shots only sped them on their way rather than bringing them down.

He stood and looked after them, wondering what their plan had been. The two had the hard-bitten look of outlaws and not the academic look of bone hunters, either in Marsh or Cope camps. Slocum approached the wagon and peered under the tarp. The bones had been bounced around but were otherwise unharmed as far as his cursory examination could determine.

"Why'd those two owlhoots stick around?" he wondered aloud. Slocum circled the wagon. The four horses in the team had not been touched. For a fleeting second, he wondered if the thieves worked for Cope. That made sense, but why hadn't they continued on their way to his camp? But if they were part of the gang of rustlers, why not take the horses and leave the wagon?

Slocum went cold inside when the answer came to him. Six men had attacked the bone-laden wagon, but only two were here. Were the others wounded by the guard's fierce defense? They might have returned to their camp to get patched up. Or perhaps they had gone to fetch someone who could determine what value lay in the wagon.

After checking the integrity of the harness, Slocum climbed into the driver's box. He avoided the spot where blood had soaked into the wooden seat, took the reins

firmly in hand and got the team moving. Slocum whistled
to his Appaloosa and let the horse trot along beside without actually tethering it to the wagon. The climb back up
the hill proved to be difficult for the team, making Slocum
wonder if this wasn't another reason the outlaws had
taken a rest. The team might have been tuckered out dragging the ton of skeletons this far.

When he reached the main road, Slocum considered his
options. Back to Marsh's camp or on to Fort Bridger? He
decided the paleontologist's camp was closer. After loading the bodies of the guard and driver into the rear of the
wagon—new bones alongside the old—he rattled and
clanked back to where the trip had begun at sunrise.

To his relief, the outlaws didn't come racing after him,
and he reached Marsh's camp at twilight to great cheers
from the workers. Their joyous cries brought Marsh and
Sanborn from the main tent.

"I got your bones," Slocum said. He glanced at the dead
driver and guard. "A couple new additions, too, I'm
afraid."

Marsh's eyes widened when he saw the dead men. Then
a storm cloud formed on his face and he began stomping
around, waving his arms like a windmill and shouting.

"I'll see him in prison, I will. Cope can't kill my best
men! He's a liar and a murderer as well as a terrible scientist."

Slocum jumped to the ground and caught up his Appaloosa's reins. He was finished with these people.

"Wait, Mr. Slocum," Marsh called. "We'll need you to
tell the marshal or sheriff or the cavalry commander that
it was Cope and his men who murdered these poor
wights."

"I don't know that was who did it," Slocum said. "The
two men I chased off might have been rustlers out for an
easy theft, or they might have been trying to figure out

what the hell they stole when they discovered nothing but bones."

"Cope did it," Marsh said firmly. "Who else?"

Slocum shrugged it off. Marsh wasn't inclined to believe the attempted theft had been nothing but a tragic mistake on the part of outlaws. If they had known what they'd stolen, Slocum would have expected a ransom note from the highwaymen. Maybe the outlaws had intended to force Marsh to bid against Cope for the bones to get the highest price possible, but that was too complicated for most owlhoots rustling cattle and stealing supplies from wagons.

"Wait, Mr. Slocum. You have done yeoman's work. Please accept my offer of employment. I have a generous grant from the university and can pay top dollar."

"Got a job already," Slocum said, thinking that Chafee must believe him long gone by now.

"I'll double whatever you are being paid to, uh, punch the cows," Marsh said.

Slocum found himself smiling, but not at the offer. Mrs. Mathiesen's cooking wasn't to be beat. He had seen how avidly Porky ate the plate of beans. If this was all that Marsh and his cook provided, Slocum would be content working for the Triple Cross for nothing but three squares a day.

"You might enjoy a new challenge, John," came Ella's teasing words.

For a second, Slocum actually considered this. Then he saw the dark look Sanborn gave him. Marsh's foreman stood directly behind Ella and glared. If Slocum accepted the job, there'd be hell to pay eventually. He slept well in the Triple Cross bunkhouse. He didn't want to sleep with one eye open watching for Sanborn to kill him in the middle of the night. Even worse, Slocum wasn't sure if Sanborn was the kind to stab him in the middle of the night while he slept. Worse, he might vent his wrath on Ella.

Slocum shook his head.

"I've got a job. You've got your bones back."

"You can stay here another night," Ella said, louder.

"Please accept the offer of the job, Mr. Slocum. I'll put you in charge of the guards. You can watch over the security of the expedition."

Slocum knew that might include some ill-conceived attack on Edward Cope and his men.

"Take a bit of advice," Slocum said, tugging on the reins and getting his Appaloosa turned around so he could mount. "Don't rile the Arapaho."

He knew Othniel Marsh wasn't likely to consider this sensible, not in his headlong rush to find every dinosaur skeleton in Wyoming. Slocum hoped Ella wouldn't get caught up in what could become a bloodbath.

7

"Well now, ain't you a sight for sore eyes," drawled Chafee when he saw Slocum riding back in to the ranch yard. "Where you been?"

"Out missing too many good meals," Slocum said, dismounting. Every muscle ached in a different fashion. He had been in the saddle too much, riding all tensed up and jumping at shadows. He wasn't sure if rustlers or Arapahos or paleontologists were going to drygulch him. He had simply ridden along with the feeling of a target drawn on his back, and it made him downright edgy.

"What'd you find out about the varmints shooting Mr. Mathiesen's cattle?" asked Chafee.

"Think I got the situation taken care of," Slocum said, fumbling in his pocket to pull out the two checks. "This ought to cover about ten of the beeves that got shot." He passed the checks to Chafee, who scowled as he worked to decipher the handwriting.

"Money from two different folks? You telling me more'n one yahoo was out there poaching on our cattle?"

"That's the size of it. Easterners," Slocum said, not keeping the contempt from his voice. "Two expeditions out hunting for old bones." He heaved a sigh and realized he didn't want to talk about it. The recitation might make him mad all over—and it certainly brought the lovely image of Ella Weedin to mind. He saw no reason to torment himself any more than necessary.

"What about the rustlers? You got a handle on them yet?" Slocum asked, wanting to forget about the two expeditions.

"You couldn't have come back at a better time. Longmeadow found where they rounded up a couple dozen head and penned them while they went after more. He thinks we can follow their trail and nab them."

"Longmeadow's still here?" asked Slocum.

"He blows hot and cold. Right now, he's thinking more about losing his pay for the month than he is on getting rich breaking his back prospecting for gold or silver." Chafee stared at the checks and laughed. "You are a caution, Slocum. I'd never have thought them scientists would have ponied up money. Hell, I'd never have thought they could shoot straight enough to kill a cow." He went off muttering to himself to turn the checks over to Mathiesen.

Slocum took the opportunity to go to the bunkhouse and splash some cold water on his face to get a bit of the trail grime off, although he knew it would be replaced soon enough by a new layer. The other cowboys milled around, talking in low tones and looking downright apprehensive.

"You heard, Slocum?" asked a sandy-haired youngster named Tatum. "About us goin' after them rustlers?"

"Chafee told me. Where's Longmeadow? If he found the trail, he might shed some light on how the rustlers operate."

"He's still back at Lightning Draw," Tatum said. "Watchin' fer any sign of them."

Slocum hadn't worked the Triple Cross long enough to know the names of the surrounding features. He dried his face on a towel hanging beside the washbasin, then rummaged through his belongings on the bottom and found some slugs and powder for his Colt. He sank to the bunk and began loading up his spare cylinders, then tucked them into a side coat pocket.

"You lookin' for a shoot-out, Mr. Slocum?" Tatum asked.

"Nope," Slocum said, "but I'm not looking to be caught napping, either." He perked up when Chafee came into the bunkhouse.

"Get saddled, men. We're going to catch us a passel of rustlers."

Chafee looked at Slocum, then glanced in Tatum's direction. Slocum understood. The foreman worried about the youngster. Still wet behind the ears, he might blunder into trouble he couldn't handle if someone didn't look after him. Slocum wanted to protest but held his tongue. He was no nursemaid, but if the foreman wanted him to keep his eyes peeled, he would.

He shrugged and then accepted the inevitable.

Chafee heaved a sigh of relief and called, "You fellows partner up. Slocum, you ride with Tatum." Chafee went around the room matching up the cowboys. He came out one shy and said, "I'll team up with Longmeadow when we get out there. No heroes, y'all hear?"

"Let's get going," Slocum said, wanting the hunt for the rustlers to be at an end as quickly as possible.

They filed out, Tatum close behind Slocum.

"Uh, Mr. Slocum," the teenager asked. "What do you think'll happen?"

"We're going to catch us some outlaws," Slocum said.

"No, I mean, well, sure, but will there be any gunplay? I'm not that good a shot, and I never shot at another man before."

"You'll do fine. Stick with me, like Chafee said." Slocum wondered if he had ever been this green, then remembered the first time he had gone into battle during the war. If it hadn't been for a corporal who had been promoted to sergeant and busted back to corporal more times than he could remember, Slocum knew he would have gotten his head blown off by federal fire the first time he went into battle.

They slung their gear on their horses and headed out, trailing after Chafee. Tatum rode at Slocum's side, looking more apprehensive with every mile they rode.

"If there's gunplay," Slocum said finally, getting a mite spooked by the boy's nervousness, "you stay back and only shoot when you're sure of your target."

"That's no good, Mr. Slocum," Tatum said. "I kin pull my own weight."

Slocum said nothing. He hoped he wouldn't get a bullet in the back of the head by mistake. Buck fever made a man shoot at anything that moved in his field of vision— and Slocum wasn't the only one likely to be drawing Tatum's fire unless the youngster settled his nerves.

"Hold up," called Chafee. "There's Longmeadow." The foreman looked at Slocum, and silent communication passed between them. Chafee wanted his best man to back him up if things turned dangerous.

Slocum rode up and asked, "Think we can leave the rest of the men behind?" He didn't mention Tatum because several others were getting a little green around the gills, too. They could face a herd of cattle in full stampede, but the notion of swapping lead with rustlers turned them into puling cowards.

"No choice." Chafee called out his orders, then trotted off with Slocum at his shoulder.

"Glad you made it so quick," Longmeadow said. He had a wild look about him that Slocum didn't like. Worse, he had picked a poor spot to wait for the rest of the cowboys from the Triple Cross to catch up. Slocum saw why this was called Lightning Draw. Steep rock faces rose almost vertically on either side. What vegetation had ever grown from those rocky faces had long since been burned off.

Slocum let Chafee talk it out with Longmeadow. He was more interested in studying the cliffs. If he had to set up an ambush, this would be the spot. A rider going into the draw would be a sitting duck for a man with a rifle on the rim. Worse, a half dozen men with rifles could take an entire company of cavalry from there. Slocum had seen how the Apaches wiped out the bluecoats time and again in Dog Canyon, down in West Texas, using this tactic.

"Straight ahead. They got a camp. About six or eight of 'em," Longmeadow rattled on. "We kin take 'em. Swoop on down and—"

"We'd have to take them by surprise," Chafee said. "They're used to handling guns, and our boys aren't." The foreman heaved a deep sigh as he thought. "We don't stand much chance in a fight," he decided. "We ought to fetch the cavalry from the fort."

"They'll be gone soon," Longmeadow said, almost frantically. "You got to take them now."

"Why are you so anxious to throw lead at them?" Slocum asked.

His eyes flickered upward and caught movement above just as Longmeadow went for his six-shooter. Longmeadow wore his pistol on his right hip and found it awkward drawing while mounted. Slocum's cross-draw holster made his six-gun easily accessible. He cleared leather and fired before Longmeadow could get his smoke wagon rolling.

The cowboy threw up his hands as the six-shooter slid from his nerveless fingers, but the damage had been done. Longmeadow going for his gun had been the signal for the rest of the rustlers lurking along the sides of the draw. A full dozen rifles spat lead. Longmeadow had even lied about the number.

"Get back, back!" shouted Slocum, firing up at the outlaws. A handgun against rifles at this range was foolhardy and a waste of ammo, but Slocum had to give Chafee the chance to figure out what was going on and then get the hell out of there.

The foreman was a smart man, but he hesitated when he saw Tatum and the rest of his cowboys galloping toward them, waving their guns in the air.

"No, go back, it's a trap!" Chafee shouted. Those were the last words he ever uttered. A rifle slug caught him in the side of the head. He slumped, blood flowing in a gory fountain from the wound, then slid slowly from horseback to lay in a pile on the ground.

Slocum cursed as he holstered his Colt Navy, then drew his Winchester. He was a good shot, a damned good one thanks to the years he had spent as a sniper during the war, but the range was great and shooting uphill was always tricky. He sent a couple of the bushwhackers scurrying for cover, but the rest continued their deadly rain.

Another of the Triple Cross riders hit the ground and lay still. Yet another yelped as a bullet grazed his thigh, forcing him to drop his six-gun.

"Get back!" Slocum ordered. "Tatum, get them out of here. We're all going to be killed if you don't." Slocum had pegged the boy right. He might not be much in the way of a marksman, but he followed orders without question. As if he herded strays, Tatum cut the rest of the Triple Cross cowboys off from the draw and drove them away while Slocum laid down a covering fire.

By the time the men were safely out of range, the fight was over. Slocum saw the rustlers fade away. They had tried to wipe out all of Mathiesen's men in one bold move and had failed.

Slocum looked down on Longmeadow's body, glanced over at Chafee and then back to the traitor. Slocum spat on his corpse, then tended to the foreman, draping his cooling body over the Appaloosa's rump and riding from what had almost been his own grave site.

"Take Chafee," he ordered Tatum. "You get them back to the ranch and tell Mr. Mathiesen what's happened."

"He's dead," Tatum said in a low voice. For a moment Slocum thought the youngster was going to cry, but he showed iron resolve. He straightened and looked Slocum square in the eye and said, "You can count on me. What are you going to do?"

"I'm going after them." Slocum judged the best way around Lightning Draw, then said, "Be sure to tell Mr. Mathiesen that Chafee died doing his job."

"I will. And I won't neglect to tell him about Longmeadow, either." The edge in Tatum's voice showed he had no more truck with a turncoat than did Slocum.

The boy shouted orders and assembled the rest of the men, all older but willing to do as they were told as long as it meant they weren't going to get their hides shot full of bullet holes. By the time Tatum was out of sight, Slocum had hit the trail and circled to the north, looking for the rustlers' camp.

He hadn't expected to find it and he didn't. Longmeadow had been bought off by the outlaws, probably after Chafee refused to let him get his pay until the rest of the men got theirs. Slocum did not care what the double-crosser's motives were. The man had paid for his treachery with his life.

The rest of the gang would pay, too, when Slocum found them. He had no illusion about taking them out one by one. He might have to be content with sending for the cavalry, as Chafee had suggested before he was shot down, but Slocum was going to see them all swing from a gallows for killing a decent, hardworking man. Slocum had liked Chafee.

A deliberate circuit around the draw revealed a trail a blind man could follow. Slocum wondered if this might be another trap, then threw caution to the wind. He rode hard in an attempt to overtake the rustlers before they made their getaway. They might be returning to their actual camp or possibly heading to where they penned the stolen beeves. If the latter, that meant they were hightailing it out of the territory.

That made it all the more important that Slocum catch them.

But as he rode, a cold knot formed in his belly. He knew where this trail led.

The rustlers rode straight as an arrow for Othniel Marsh's camp.

8

Slocum took the time to knock out the cylinder from his Colt and replace it with a loaded one from his coat pocket. As he worked, he turned grimmer by the second. He hadn't taken much of a shine to Professor Marsh, but he hadn't thought the man would be in cahoots with cold-blooded, murderous rustlers.

But the paleontologist had shown his innate fierceness whenever he spoke of Edward Cope. Put the two men in a room and only one would come out alive.

That didn't bother Slocum as much as the notion that Marsh had hired the rustlers to stir up trouble. They certainly could provide a steady flow of fresh meat for his expedition, and might even be useful as guards. Slocum had not bothered to pay much attention to the hard cases watching over the camp, and the only one he had seen close-up was the dead guard on the bone wagon.

He shoved his six-shooter back into the holster and continued along the trail, riding straight into Marsh's camp.

Slocum's green eyes bored into every nook and cranny, looking for the rustlers. The ground was so cut up by heavy wagons and other horses that he lost track of the rustlers' hoofprints. But they had ridden to the edge of camp. That was good enough for Slocum to pursue them, wherever it led him.

"Mr. Slocum, you're back," Professor Marsh called, looking up from a table where he pored over a stack of small bones. "I trust you've chosen to accept my offer of employment."

"Where are they?" Slocum demanded. He expected to see a dozen rifle barrels poke out from the tents, all trained on him. If that happened, the rustlers would find that taking him down was a lot harder than shooting Chafee from the saddle.

"My researchers? Why, they chose to follow the stratum in the rock and—"

"The rustlers," Slocum said harshly. "I trailed them to your camp. Where are they?"

"Rustlers? I do not understand."

Slocum saw Sanborn bustling over, a pickax in his hand and a look of pure malice on his face. Sliding to the ground, Slocum walked over to Marsh's foreman and, before Sanborn could say a word, unloaded a haymaker that sent him stumbling back to sit down hard. Sanborn looked stunned.

"The rustlers killed a friend of mine. He was foreman at the Triple Cross, and they're not getting away with it. Where are they?"

"I know nothing of any rustlers. I thought we had settled the matter of my, uh, exuberance in shooting native wildlife."

"You shot the cattle. They stole a hundred head or more and killed Chafee."

"You keep saying that. I tell you, Mr. Slocum, I know nothing of rustlers." Marsh stood and looked vexed. Slocum turned on him and drew his six-gun, cocked it and pointed it at the professor's face.

"Where are they? This is your last chance to tell me."

"John! Stop, wait!" Ella came rushing from a nearby tent, but she wasn't going to deter him.

"Time's up." Slocum's finger tightened on the trigger and then relaxed when Ella jumped between Marsh and the muzzle of the Colt.

"Have you gone mad?" she cried. "Othniel doesn't know anything about rustlers or murderers!"

"Except Cope," the professor said, banging on his usual drum. "I'd expect anything from him. He's treacherous, that one. And a poor scholar."

"Shut up," Slocum said.

"You can't talk that way to the professor!" Sanborn had regained his feet and came for Slocum. This time Slocum laid him low by forcefully laying the Colt's barrel alongside his head.

"John, please. What's going on?" Ella looked vexed rather than scared, and this let Slocum simmer a mite.

"I tracked rustlers to this camp. Where are they?"

"We don't know anything about them," Ella said. "The only men who've come into camp were two diggers and Sanborn, and they showed up just after sunrise. Since then no one's left and there certainly have *not* been any cattle thieves entering camp."

Slocum considered her words. The trail had been confused at the edge of camp. He had no proof the rustlers had actually come into camp rather than skirting it on their way elsewhere. Something else bothered him, too, and this uncertainty caused him to lower the hammer on his six-gun and finally return the weapon to its holster.

"That's better," Ella said. "You should be ashamed of yourself causing such fright."

"Cope's the one you want," Marsh called, not the least cowed by any threat Slocum had made. Slocum pegged the man as a fool if he didn't know death when it stared him in the face.

Then pieces fell together—and his theory fell apart.

"The wagon filled with bones," he said. "If the rustlers killed the guard and driver, that means the guard wasn't one of their gang."

"What?" Ella looked confused, but Slocum plowed on, getting details straight in his own mind.

"If the rustlers stole the wagon, thinking it was carrying supplies, that meant they didn't have anyone in camp to tell them the real cargo."

"That's so," Ella said. "Now are you convinced the rustlers aren't lurking among us?"

Slocum looked at Sanborn, who again got to his feet. The man wobbled as he took a few steps. His right eye was swelled shut and his lip was cut. Slocum refrained from hitting him again, just to vent some of his bile.

"If you chased them this far, you ought to continue after them," Othniel Marsh said. "But mark my words, Cope is behind it. He could have hired them to create a fracas to draw your attention to my worthy work and away from his pilfering ways. If a man can steal another's research, he can steal a few noisy cows."

Slocum took his time studying the camp and saw no place where a dozen rustlers on the run could hide. The few horses penned in a crude corral looked rested and well tended, not like horses almost run into the ground getting here from Lightning Draw. The rustlers probably had circled the camp to leave a confusing trail.

"Look to Cope, Mr. Slocum. If there's any perfidy afoot, he is the cause," Marsh said with great conviction.

"I'll keep after them. You guard your supplies," Slocum warned. "Those rustlers might be on their way out of the territory, or they might think there's nothing that can stop them. Any gang nervy enough to lay an ambush for all a rancher's cowboys is capable of about anything."

Slocum had turned to mount when Marsh called to him, "The offer of a job still stands, Mr. Slocum. I can use your particular skills."

"Yes," said Ella, grinning her infectious grin, "you've actually shut up Sanborn for a few minutes. That's quite an accomplishment."

"We can talk after I run those sons of bitches to ground," Slocum said. Marsh gaped at the use of such coarse language in front of a lady, but Ella only laughed.

Slocum rode to the point where he had lost the definite trail, then began circling the camp. A quarter of the way around he again picked up the rustlers' trail. He wondered how so many men had ridden this near the camp with no one noticing; then he figured the scientists were too consumed by their hunt for dinosaur bones. A cannon could have gone off and no one would have noticed anything out of the ordinary.

Slocum quickly came to the end of the easily visible trail. Cursing, he dropped to the ground and began studying the earth for the small signs of passage. The rustlers had uprooted bushes and now dragged them behind on the softer section of the trail, but worse for Slocum, they sought out the rocky stretches. Tracking became harder and harder, until he was forced to give up, as the sun began dipping behind the Wasatch Mountains far to the west.

As he pitched camp, Slocum heard distant hoofbeats. He left his bedroll where he had flung it next to a small cooking fire, grabbed his rifle and sought out a suitable juniper for cover. Cocking the rifle, he settled the barrel in a notch formed by two misshapen limbs and waited.

Twilight had settled in and began turning to inky night, but Slocum saw the indistinct figure approaching. He centered the rider in his sights. His finger slowly squeezed, then he released quickly when he heard Ella Weedin call out.

"Where are you, John? I know you're here somewhere. I followed you all day."

"What are you doing out here?" he asked, coming from

behind the tree. She rode closer, then bent over and stared at him.

"You were going to shoot me," she said, a hint of astonishment in her voice. "Did you think I was a rustler?"

"I didn't know who you were. You were supposed to stay in camp."

"Why? I'm a free spirit. I can roam where I choose," she said, dismounting. As she dismounted, Slocum caught sight of Ella's fine legs. He should send her back immediately, but he knew he wouldn't.

"Why did your free spirit decide to float this direction?" he asked. "Not that I'm complaining."

"You shouldn't," she said almost primly. The woman's auburn locks drifted like a mist around her pale oval face, and her blue eyes glowed with a fierce inner light that set Slocum's heart racing. "I figured it out. Those men—the rustlers—must work for Cope. Wait!" she said, holding up her hand. "I'm not repeating something Othniel told me, far from it. It makes sense that Cope hired them."

"Why's that?" he asked.

"They stole the wagon of fossils being sent to Fort Bridger, but you stopped them before they could turn the cargo over to Cope."

"Maybe," Slocum said. "That doesn't change the fact these gents are stealing Triple Cross cattle."

"They might be working for themselves most of the time, then doing odd jobs for Cope. He is not above stealing a shipment of dinosaur skeletons and claiming them for his own. He's done worse."

She walked to the fire and kicked a few extra logs onto it. The sudden blaze caused sparks to twist and turn like demented fireflies soaring into the sky.

"There, that's better," she said.

"Better for what? Not for cooking. The flames are too high unless you want boiled coffee and burnt beans."

"Better for what?" she mocked. "I do not intend to

freeze." She slipped off her blouse and cast it aside, waiting for his reaction. A slow smile came to Slocum's lips. He had suspected she had something like this in mind.

Without another word, she unfastened her riding skirt and stepped out of it, then bent and spread out his bedroll. As she bent, she thrust her perky behind up and stretched her frilly undergarments tight. Slocum moved around the fire and came in behind her. He reached out and stroked over the taut flesh he felt under the fabric.

Dropping to his knees while she remained bent over, he found luscious, warm flesh under the cloth and began moving upward. His fingers stroked and teased as he moved ever higher. By the time his hand brushed across the fleecy triangle hidden between her thighs, the woman quivered with need. She let out a sharp gasp when his finger invaded her and began moving about slowly, rotating and then slipping in and out.

"So nice, John," she sobbed out, "but I want something more there. More. More of what you have to offer."

She hiked her underskirts and exposed the gleaming half moons of her rump. Slocum bent forward and kissed her, first on the left cheek and then on the right. Ella widened her stance as Slocum twisted around under her and came up between her legs. His mouth pressed firmly into the furred, tangled nest he had just explored with his finger. This time his tongue shot forth, battered wetly past her nether lips and sank sinuously into her.

A new shiver passed through the woman, robbing her of strength. Ella began sinking down, pressing Slocum to the ground under her until she was spread above him. He kept up the oral assault, teasing and tormenting until he found the tiny pink spire at the top of her womanly crease. He sucked this between his lips and flicked the tip of his tongue back and forth until the shivers in Ella's body turned into a monstrous earthquake.

For a moment he was delightfully deaf and blind, surrounded by her tensed legs.

The spasm passed and Ella collapsed onto the bedroll.

"You're not through, are you?" he teased. Slocum rolled over and sat up, removing his vest, shirt and gunbelt quickly. Even working as fast as he had, it wasn't quick enough for the lusty woman. She already had his jeans unfastened and dug about in the front to get out his rigid organ.

"Yes," she said. "This is what I want—run it through me, John. Give every last inch of it to me."

He silenced her with kisses and bore her flat onto her back. Her warm, firm breasts crushed against his broad chest as they kissed. Then he began working down to her chin, along her jawline, lavishing kisses as he went. His tongue flicked lightly at her earlobe, mimicking the action done earlier and lower. By the time he kissed her neck, she had repositioned herself under him. Her legs spread wantonly, and she lifted herself upward off the blanket to grind her crotch into his, putting into action what she desired most.

Slocum lifted himself on his arms and looked down into her face, wondering if any angel could be prettier. Her breasts quaked. He saw the chilly night air that she had tried to fend off with a bigger fire had now turned her nipples to hard little pink pebbles. Each was given a kiss, a lick and then a tiny nip that caused Ella to groan with pleasure.

By now Slocum was responding fully to the way her inner thighs rose and stroked along the sides of his body. He moved forward, positioned himself and then slipped gradually into her heated core. Inch by slow inch he entered her, not responding to her fevered cries for more speed. Only when he was fully in her clutching, clinging moist female tunnel did he pause.

Sweat beaded Slocum's face and trickled down his

chest. The breeze whipping up turned them into cold spears that contrasted mightily with the heat in his crotch. He began rotating his hips slowly, going first in one direction and then the other. Ella gasped, sobbed and begged. He refused to go faster.

Until he felt his own uncontrollable heat begin to rise. Slocum retreated until only the tip of his manhood remained within, then slid forward. This time he moved faster, with more determination, with greater need.

He rolled her back as her legs went higher. Snaring one shapely ankle, he draped it over his shoulder. Then he caught the other and bent Ella almost double as he sank back into her—pulled ever deeper by ancient instincts.

"Yes, oh, yes, John. I—aieee!" The woman shook like a leaf caught in a tornado. She shivered and trembled and collapsed around Slocum's hidden stalk.

He swallowed hard, felt more sweat trickle down his chest and then looked at her passion-seized face. No angel looked like this. Ella was angel and devil, all in one. Slocum swung his hips back and then began stroking with powerful movements that built such carnal heat that it threatened to burn Slocum to a nub.

He was past caring. His entire soul focused on the woman and the pleasure boiling in his—in their—loins. Faster. He moved faster. Heat exploded within him and spread throughout his body. Faster, ever faster, deeper, harder.

He erupted as a new orgasm possessed Ella. Locked together, they rocked through the ultimate in pleasurable human sensation. Spent, Slocum straightened and released her legs, letting them down gently on either side. He stretched out on the woman, his weight still pinning her to the ground.

"You can lie beside me," she said, struggling under his bulk.

"Nope," he said. "This way you won't run off."

"There's no chance of that," Ella said with feeling. "Why do you think I'd do a foolish thing like that?" She stroked over his muscled back and down until she cupped his rock-hard buttocks.

"You're so damn beautiful you have to be a mirage."

Ella laughed delightedly at the compliment. Then she proved to him there was no chance she would vanish.

9

"Who else could it be, John?" Ella Weedin asked. She idly ran her fingers through the mat of hair on Slocum's bare chest, then looked up, her guileless blue eyes rivaling the cloudless Wyoming sky for beauty.

"You could be right," he allowed. "Cope seems to be quite a scoundrel, but then Marsh isn't lily-pure himself."

"He knows what he's doing. The man is a genius, John, and a little bit different from you and me."

"I don't know. You showed quite a bit of genius last night," he said, laughing.

"Not that kind of genius, silly," she said, swatting him. "At least not any kind I'd know. Othniel Marsh keeps to himself a lot. His thoughts keep him too occupied for any other distractions."

"His loss," Slocum said. "I like your expert behavior." He bantered with her but found himself distracted as he turned over in his mind everything Ella had told him about Cope. The other expedition leader might have hired the rustlers to do some dirty work for him, but Cope wasn't their leader. Rustlers focused on stealing cattle, not bones. If Cope offered a few extra dollars, the outlaws would take his money but would always return to the crime that they knew the best. By now, the rustlers must have a couple hundred head of Mathiesen's beeves ready to run to market.

"How about this?" Ella asked. "We sneak over to Cope's camp and watch him for a spell. If you see the rustlers or I spot anything else that looks as if he is responsible for Marsh's recent losses, then we can decide what to do."

"I'll turn him over to the cavalry," Slocum said, though he preferred the idea of stringing up the murdering thieves from the nearest sturdy tree limb. Chafee had been a good man. "They're not doing their job in these parts, not with the rustlers running free the way they are."

"Then it's settled. We go to Cope's camp."

"I go to his camp. It's too dangerous for you to come along if he's hired the rustlers to be his personal highbinders."

"How would you identify the skeletons that have been stolen from Marsh? I know what they look like. Why, I sketched most of them!"

"All right, but we don't do anything if he has the dinosaur bones. Understand?"

"Cross my heart, I'll be good," she said, sitting up and letting the blanket fall from her bare chest. She flashed him her wicked grin and then said, "And after I've stopped being good, then I'll be naughty."

"Get dressed," Slocum said. He watched as she lithely stood and pranced around camp buck naked. He cared nothing about Marsh's dry bones when he could get a gander at Ella's fine skeleton. Reluctantly, he heaved himself up and climbed into his clothes. The dinosaur bones meant nothing, but the cattle meant the difference between a profitable year and going broke for Mathiesen and the Triple Cross Ranch.

They rode until Slocum got his bearings. He kept his eye on the ground, hunting for any sign of the gang of rustlers, but they had hidden their trail well before. If they had come this way, they'd done even better making certain no one picked up their spoor.

"Just on the other side of this hill," Slocum said, studying the grassy slope leading to the ridge. This part of Wyoming tended toward flat, but the occasional hill turned into an unexpected mountain. Cope had chosen a spot for his excavation stretching from the other face of the hill across the prairie.

"How do we proceed, John?" The gentle, warm breeze mussed Ella's hair even more than it was from the ride, and reddened her cheeks, giving her a slightly flushed look. If anything, she was even lovelier than she had been the night before.

Slocum didn't answer right away. He was too busy hunting for any sign that more than a rider or two had come this way. For all he could find, the rustlers had simply vanished into thin air after they had laid their false trail to Marsh's camp the day before.

He tilted his head back and sniffed hard at the wind blowing down from the hill. Then he listened and made a full circle, his sharp green eyes missing nothing.

"Nobody's been on this side of the hill in a while."

"Perhaps there are no bone fields worth excavating here," Ella said.

Slocum was continually amazed at the members of both expeditions and their preoccupation with a pile of bones from improbable animals. He wasn't certain he believed Marsh when he said those skeletons were from creatures living millions of years earlier, any more than he was sure that Ella's sketches mirrored the beasts that had left those bones behind.

"I was hunting for any trace of the rustlers," he told her. He looked up the hill and came to a decision. "We can do worse than hike up there and sit in the shade of that scrub oak."

He started climbing, leading his Appaloosa. Ella was a tad slower to come along but did. She cautiously poked her head up when they reached the ridge, and looked down into Cope's camp.

"Why, we can see wonderfully well from here!"

"Tether the horses and sit down," Slocum said. "Unless we move around a lot, they'll never notice us up here."

"How wonderful," she said. Ella took a small sketch pad from her saddlebags and sat with her back to the smooth-barked oak and began sketching what she could see of Cope's bone reconstructions below. Slocum settled down and slowly surveyed the other scientist's camp. For the life of him, Slocum couldn't see any evidence that the outlaws had come this way and were in Cope's camp.

After a while, in spite of the distance robbing most of the detail, Slocum fancied he could pick out Edward Cope and his foreman. It took him a couple seconds to remember the man's name. Leigh. They went about the business of digging out the bones and never gave a hint of doing anything illegal.

"John!" Ella sat bolt upright and pointed. For a moment, he thought she had spotted the rustlers. But that wasn't what had drawn her attention. It was a collection of bleached white bones out back of Cope's tent. "Those are Othniel's! Cope has stolen them. I know it!"

"How can you tell?" To Slocum they looked exactly like any other bone pile around the camp. Some of these had been loosely wired together and stretched what looked to be five feet along the ground, but without many of the ribs attached to the spine.

"Professor Marsh was the first to discover that particular species of dinosaur," Ella said angrily. "Cope's taken it! Othniel would never have *given* those bones to his greatest rival."

Slocum had to admit she was right on this point. Put Cope and Marsh in the same room and only one would walk out. That did nothing to answer a more pressing question. Had Cope hired the rustlers? Slocum cared less about bone theft than he did rustled cattle. If Cope had hired the outlaws, he knew where their hideout was. And if he didn't, he had some way of contacting them. That might be as good as getting a map to their hideout.

Slocum could send a bogus message and lure them out. If the cavalry was waiting, they could sweep up the entire pile of dirt.

But he saw nothing in Cope's camp to indict the paleontologist.

"I'm going to demand that he return those bones," Ella said, getting to her feet and brushing herself off. "How dare he take a valuable specimen like that!"

"Hold your horses," Slocum said, reaching out and grabbing the furious woman by the arm. He pulled her back down. "Don't go showing your hand yet. Are you sure those bones belong to Marsh?"

"I am," she said. "I've got sketches somewhere. Here. Here they are! See?" Ella leafed through a dozen sheets before finding one of some strange foxlike creature. Slocum looked from the drawing to the bones and back. For the life of him, he saw no similarity.

"When did you do this sketch?" he asked.

"Weeks ago. I thought Othniel had sent the skeleton back to Yale, but obviously Cope sidetracked it. That crook probably bribed someone on the train to mark it as sent when it was actually sitting on a siding somewhere."

"Is there any way of verifying that's Marsh's property?" Slocum asked.

"What do you think it is, John? A dinosaur skeleton doesn't come with a deed to it. There might be some chip marks, but identifying them would be hard. The professor would have to do that himself."

Slocum stewed as he sat and glared at Cope, Leigh and the rest of the workmen toiling in their excavation. He saw no evidence of rustlers, but Ella claimed that heap of bones had been stolen. If he could prove Cope had swiped the bones, he might get enough leverage against the man to find out about the rustlers.

"We can wait until dark and then go down and get a closer look," Slocum said.

"And?" she prodded.

"Then we'll decide what to do," Slocum said. He leaned back, tipped down the brim of his hat and tried to sleep. Being alert when it came time to sneak into Cope's camp was important, but it took him a long, long while before he drifted off.

When Slocum awoke, the temperature was already dropping. He looked around and saw Ella hunkered down a few yards away, staring fixedly at Cope's camp. A few cooking fires sputtered there but mostly there was little activity.

"What's happened?" Slocum asked.

"Cope, Leigh and several others rode out in a hurry about an hour ago when a courier came in with a message."

"Courier? What'd he look like?" Slocum came instantly awake. This might be the break he needed if the rider with the urgent summons came from the rustlers' camp.

Ella shrugged and said nothing. From this distance, he doubted that she had gotten a good look at the man. It had taken Slocum the better part of an hour of careful observation to pick out the distinct mannerisms of Cope and his foreman, so he couldn't fault her for not providing a detailed description. It would have been vindication, however, if she could have identified a rustler.

"I'm going to the camp to poke around," Slocum said, coming to a decision.

"I'm coming, too, John," she said. "I must look at that skeleton more closely. I'm sure it's Marsh's."

"How many are left in the camp?" Slocum asked. Cope

didn't have the guards that Marsh posted. Most of his crew worked on actual digging rather than wandering about with rifles looking for intruders. With so many gone from the camp, along with their leader, the camp was wide open to his spying.

"A half dozen but no more than that," Ella said. "John, I *have* to see the skeleton."

It went against his better judgment, but Slocum curtly nodded, then set off down the hill. There was little likelihood he would be seen in the intense darkness. The sliver of moon wasn't set to rise for an hour yet. By then Slocum intended to be long gone, either with evidence tying Cope and the rustlers together, or with enough assurance that the scientist had nothing to do with the cattle thefts to safely ignore him.

Stones skittered away from their boots as they half walked, half slid down the hill, but Slocum kept a close watch on the shapes around the campfires. Nobody heard them, in spite of the racket.

"There, John. I need to study it," Ella said. She tugged at him to go to the skeleton they had spotted behind Cope's tent.

"You go. I need to satisfy myself all's on the up-and-up," he told her. She heaved a deep breath, then hurried to examine the pile of bones.

Slocum wondered if she would be all right, then pushed it from his mind and went to check the chuck wagon. Careful not to rattle the pots and pans dangling down, he rummaged through Cope's larder until he was certain he wasn't missing anything. If Cope had anything to do with the rustlers, he was getting cheated. Maggoty bacon and salt pork with mold growing on it were the only slabs of meat. Slocum's mouth watered as he remembered the thick steaks Mrs. Mathiesen had served. Triple Cross beef wasn't to be missed.

Nowhere else did Slocum find any hint that the rustlers

had been in Cope's camp. Moving on cat's feet, he walked past a man who might have been stationed as a sentry but now dozed, bearded chin bumping against his chest every time he breathed. Slocum ducked into Cope's tent, made a cursory examination of papers on a small writing desk and saw only detailed drawings and crabbed handwriting in a leather-bound diary describing what the sketches meant.

No evidence of dealings with the rustlers.

Slocum slipped out and went to join Ella. She ran her fingers over the skeleton, as she had done his flesh the night before. The expression on her face was similar. Whatever the fever Othniel Marsh had for these bones, Ella Weedin shared it.

"This is so beautiful, John," she said, seeing him come up. "And it's Marsh's. Cope stole it!"

"That'll give the soldiers something to think about," Slocum said. He wasn't sure what law Cope violated by stealing bones found in the ground. Just because Marsh had found them first didn't make them his. "Let's get out of here."

"What? No!" she cried. He clapped a hand over her mouth to muffle any more outbursts. Ella mumbled and Slocum released her. "We have to take it back. It's not right letting Cope keep this, John."

He looked at the skeleton. It was partially wired together, but most of the bones that apparently fit on somewhere were in two burlap bags.

"We can't take it with us."

"Yes, we can. I can carry the bags. You can get the skeleton."

Slocum was astounded at her suggestion. Ella sounded serious. Then he saw she wasn't kidding when she hefted the two bags, staggering a little under their combined weight.

"Well, go on, get the rest," she said.

Slocum wrapped his arms around the skeleton and lifted. It was heavier than he expected and much bulkier. Worse, it was awkward to carry, with pieces flopping and clacking about. He made so much noise he worried even the sleepy guard would hear and come to see what the commotion was.

Then he got a better grip and started after the already retreating woman. Slocum followed her up the hill, wondering if he did right helping her recover the skeleton.

If it even had been taken in the first place. There was no way for him to know. Worse than the possibility he was stealing another man's property, Slocum knew he was throwing kerosene into the fire already blazing between Cope and Marsh.

10

John Slocum rode slowly back to the Triple Cross, thinking hard about returning the dinosaur skeleton to Marsh.
The burr under his saddle was beginning to fester—was
that skeleton ever Marsh's property? Slocum's gut told
him that Ella Weedin had duped him into stealing the
product of Edward Cope's hard work.

Marsh's reaction on seeing the bones convinced Slocum that the paleontologist had never laid eyes on them
before. The professor had gushed over the uniqueness of
the specimen and run his fingers over the fossil like he
was caressing a lover's cheek. A new lover's cheek. Ella
quickly reassured Slocum that Cope had swiped the
bones, but Marsh never agreed with her on this point. He
immediately took the bones to his assembly area, studying
each fragment and working to fit it together, lost in his
own world and deaf to questions Slocum posed.

Nothing Slocum had done in the past couple days
amounted to a hill of beans, and he had seen a good man
killed, to boot.

"Hey, Mr. Slocum, we didn't think you was comin'
back." Tatum popped from the bunkhouse like he was on

fire when Slocum drew rein in front of the main house. He stood, staring up eagerly at Slocum.

"Had to come back to be sure they got Chafee buried," Slocum said.

"We buried him right up there, on the hill lookin' down over the whole danged range," Tatum said. The youngster shifted his weight nervously.

"What is it?" Slocum asked sharply. He was in no mood to mince words.

"I'd sure like to be the outrider this week. That section of land to the north, the grassland by the river, I kin get through it like a dose of salts. Won't be a single stray out there I don't find."

"Why are you asking me?" Slocum looked at the eager youth.

"You're the new foreman. Mr. Mathiesen got out of his sickbed this morning and said so this morning. Nobody put up a bit of fuss over it, neither," Tatum said proudly. "We all know you got experience, maybe the most of any of us."

"The devil you say." Slocum dragged his saddle off the Appaloosa and settled it over a rail. He looked toward the bunkhouse and saw some of the cowboys peering out the door, waiting for him to give them orders. Slocum had intended to ride west and to hell with Marsh and Cope and rustlers willing to ambush a good man like Chafee.

Before Tatum could say another word, Slocum stalked to the main house and went up the steps to knock at the main door.

"Slocum, come on in. We got to talk," said Mr. Mathiesen, propped up with pillows on the sofa in his parlor. Slocum hesitated, hat clutched in his hand. The ranch owner looked twenty years older than he had only a week earlier. The strain of running the Triple Cross Ranch was wearing him down like wood pushed repeatedly against a grinding stone. Slocum fancied he could see the sharp splinters poking out of the man as he fell apart.

Slocum spent the next hour with Mathiesen and eventually emerged into the bright sunlight, a little disgusted with himself for agreeing to replace Chafee as foreman. But the pay he had been offered was a decent wage, and Slocum would track down the rustlers responsible for Chafee's death with Mathiesen's blessing. If the law couldn't do anything about that, he would.

"All right, gather round," Slocum called, getting the cowhands out of their bunks and on their feet. They had never been all that friendly toward him, and now it paid off. It never paid for a foreman to get too cozy with his crew. It undermined authority. "Chafee's pushing up daisies and Mr. Mathiesen put me in his job. I didn't want it, so if any of you think you can do the job, speak up and it's yours." Slocum looked around the small circle of faces. Some were disgusted, more were resigned, and only a couple were bright and excited. Tatum was one of those.

"Anything you want, Mr. Slocum, we'll jump to it," Tatum said.

"Which of you knew Longmeadow best?" Slocum saw poker faces go on, but one man at the back averted his eyes and tried to vanish. Being built like a brick shithouse, he didn't do such a good job. Slocum went up to him and looked up an inch or two into the man's face.

"I didn't know him, not that good. Look, Slocum," the man blurted, "I had nuthin' to do with Longmeadow throwin' in with the rustlers!"

"Never said you did," Slocum said in a level voice. "If I thought you knew anything about it, I wouldn't be talking. I'd be shooting."

The man's face drained of color, and his eyes went wide with fright.

"Longmeadow found them somewhere on the range. You have any idea where?"

"Might be that he ran into one or two of them varmints

at Fort Bridger. The saloon's wide-open territory. Not much in the way of law."

"There's a federal marshal up north a ways in Kemmerer, and of course there's the cavalry post outside town. Fort Bridger, it's called, too, but it's separate from the trading post by a couple miles," supplied Tatum. Slocum ignored Tatum's anxious flood of information and kept the big cowboy fixed by his penetrating gaze.

"So Longmeadow talked to one or two rustlers in town," Slocum said. "What did he tell you about it? Didn't he ask you to throw in with him?"

"I . . . no, yes, well, he never actually asked me to double-cross Mr. Mathiesen. Mathiesen's been good to me. To all of us. It was Chafee who wouldn't give Longmeadow his wages."

"Where?" Slocum asked.

It took a few more minutes of badgering, but Slocum finally got a decent description of where Longmeadow had joined the rustlers.

"Listen up. None of you'll go after the rustlers. Too dangerous. You do your work, you stay out of trouble, you get paid." Slocum took a deep breath to clear his head. He got a moment's giddiness from talking to the men as he had spoken to reb soldiers during the war. He had been a captain but had never liked the idea of sending men into battle to die. More than once, he had been at the forefront of the attack, doing what he had ordered his men to do.

He had come through the war. Many of his subordinates hadn't, because of orders he had given.

Slocum put his hand on his belly, over the scar left after Bloody Bill Anderson had gut-shot him for protesting the killing of boys as young as eight during Quantrill's raid on Lawrence, Kansas. That wound was the worst he had sustained, and it had been inflicted by someone supposedly on the same side of the war.

No federal bullet had left as deep a scar, either physically or emotionally.

He began barking out orders, telling the men where to fix fence, where to round up strays, how to do their jobs. Chafee had been a good man but a lax one when it came to keeping the cowboys in line.

"Everyone knows what he's supposed to do," Slocum said. "So do it!"

The men let out a small cheer that startled him. They hurried off to get into the saddle and do their work, all save Tatum.

"You're goin' after them rustlers," the young man said. "Let me watch your back, Mr. Slocum."

"Not satisfied being outrider today?" Slocum asked.

"Oh, no, that was real good of you to let me show what I can do, but that was before you wormed that about Longmeadow out of Fallon. They weren't that good of friends, but if anyone knew anything, it'd be Fallon."

"Think you could be foreman?" Slocum asked, taking Tatum by surprise with the question.

"Someday, maybe, but not now. I got a whole lot to learn."

"The first thing to learn is don't piss me off. Get out there and do your job," Slocum said. Tatum jumped as if he had stepped on a rattler and hurried to saddle his horse.

Slocum made sure Tatum was on the way to the far side of the ranch before he gathered what supplies he thought he'd need and got his tired Appaloosa back on the trail. Giving the cowboys enough work to keep them busy for a week gave Slocum some breathing room. Nobody would ask after him, and he knew the men well enough that they wouldn't slack off. Not too much.

Even if they did, they'd leave him alone.

He wanted plenty of time to find the spot where Longmeadow had parleyed with the rustlers and then been won over by them. If this was a regular rendezvous point, Slocum figured he could find the outlaws' camp without much problem. They had already shown themselves to be masterful at concealing their trail. Might be, they wouldn't be quite so efficient if he found a spot they considered secret.

Slocum rode steadily all day and finally found the ravine Fallon had described. Coming off a considerable elevation, spring runoff had cut a deep arroyo covered with sand, gravel and pebbles as large as his thumbnail. Walking his horse in the sandy bottom tired the Appaloosa quickly, and Slocum soon discovered he wasn't likely to find any tracks this way. The shifting sand and rocky crust didn't take hoofprints easily.

Using his skills, Slocum found himself returning to stare at a stand of trees a quarter mile up the arroyo, no matter what else he studied.

He gave in to instinct and ducked under the low-hanging branches to find a small watering hole and evidence that more than a few fires had been built here over the past few weeks. This was the perfect meeting place for rustlers. Trees protected them from view from out on the grasslands, the watering hole refreshed them and their mounts, and a canyon mouth beckoned not five miles away.

If Slocum had to hide out, that canyon was exactly the place where he would pitch camp.

By the time he had grabbed a cold meal and let his horse rest and take its fill of water, it was getting toward late afternoon. Sneaking into the rustlers' camp would be easier in the dark, but finding it after sundown was nigh on impossible.

Rested and well fed, Slocum was ready to hunt down the rustlers. He swung into the saddle and started for the mouth of the canyon. Before he had ridden half a mile, he saw poorly concealed tracks. Then he found more hoofprints that the horses' riders had done nothing to hide.

A calm settled on him like a well-worn jacket, familiar and comfortable. Slocum couldn't remember the number of times he had ridden straight into the jaws of danger.

So far, he had ridden away afterward. Slocum saw no reason to believe this was going to be any different.

The setting sun cast long shadows along the canyon floor. At the same time, anyone walking the canyon rim would be silhouetted, giving him plenty of time to avoid being seen. The only worrisome part of entering the canyon was the echo caused by his Appaloosa's hooves clacking against the stony ground. Every step reverberated like a gunshot.

Slocum cut toward one canyon wall and followed it deeper into the canyon, finding traces of cattle having been herded through here recently. He smiled mirthlessly. Not only might he bring Chafee's killers to justice, he might just recover the beeves stolen off the Triple Cross.

His nose twitched when he caught the faint scent of juniper smoke on the wind blowing out of the canyon. A cook fire? No hint of food came along with the wood smoke, putting him on guard. It was too early in the evening for a fire to keep men warm while they slept.

Slocum grabbed his rifle and slid to the ground to advance on foot. He had to find out what was going on before he barged in. Pushing through the tangled undergrowth left small cuts on his arms and body; thorny brush got thicker as he came to the edge of a clearing. Two fires burned in the center. Nothing else was in sight. No bedrolls. No horses. No chuck wagon.

No rustlers.

Slocum frowned. Someone had set those fires to blazing and had done so recently. He studied the edge of the clearing for any sign of where the men had gone. The dark woods surrounding the rocky region did not betray any trap.

He didn't hear or smell cattle, either. Penning a couple

hundred head would have produced a ruckus that could never be smothered by the soft breeze whipping down the canyon. Something wasn't right.

Slocum began circling the clearing, and finally poked through the undergrowth and stepped out to get a better feel for what had gone on. The tracks were too confused for easy reading. Slocum spiraled in to the twin fires, then stopped when he saw a single trail that had been erased using an uprooted bush.

Slocum lifted his rifle and aimed it directly into the woods.

"Drop your gun and come out!" Slocum called. His finger tensed on the trigger, ready to fire at the slightest movement in the woods.

"No, you drop you yours," came a cold voice from Slocum's right. He started to swing around and fire, but other movement seen out of the corners of his eyes told him the sorry truth.

He stood in the middle of a clearing, completely surrounded by men with guns pointing at him.

11

Slocum's mind raced to find a way out of this trap. He couldn't believe he had been so careless that he had fallen into it this easily, but there wasn't time for self-recrimination. Turning slowly, he saw no fewer than eight men, all with six-shooters pointed in his direction. But their snare had one problem, and Slocum exploited it without thinking.

Diving forward, he fired his rifle, hit the ground, rolled and fired behind him. The men were in a circle, their weapons pointed inward—and across the clearing at their partners standing opposite.

Eight six-guns blazed, sending lead flying wildly all around. Slocum added to it with a few well-placed shots, but he was less interested in winging or killing his attackers than he was in getting away without weighing a pound or two more from lead added to his body by their fierce gunfire.

"Stop firing, dammit! He's gettin' away!" shouted the man who had ordered Slocum to throw down his rifle. "You're shootin' at each other. Stop shootin'!"

To Slocum's surprise, the men obeyed instantly. He dug his toes in and tried to reach the dubious shelter of the thorny bushes he had pushed aside to get into the clearing.

A bullet blew splinters off the tree in front of him, forcing him to duck and dodge. A second slug tore the heel off his boot, sending him stumbling into the bushes. Slocum instinctively threw his arms up to protect his face, and lost his rifle.

Then it was over. Before he could rip free of the inch-long thorns slashing at his flesh, four men pointed their six-shooters at him from point-blank range.

"You got me," he said, wondering why the rustlers wanted to take him prisoner. An intruder ought to be cut down and left for the coyotes.

"Where's the rest of your gang?" demanded the man in charge. He swaggered over, spinning his six-shooter by the trigger guard around his index finger. With a smooth move, he rolled the pistol around and returned it to his holster.

"The rest?" Slocum asked, not wanting to give away that he had foolishly blundered into the camp by himself. "Waiting to swoop in and string up the lot of you murderers." He wanted to play for time. All he needed was a small lapse and he might turn the tables.

Maybe. When hell froze over.

"You got that backwards, boy," the man said, coming around. Slocum's eyes narrowed when he saw a shiny badge pinned on the man's vest, barely visible behind his coat. "We're gonna string *you* up for all the rustling you been doin'."

"I'm not a rustler," Slocum said. "You're a federal marshal?"

"Deputy marshal," the man said, pulling back his coat to display his badge fully.

"This here's Deputy Gaines. He's the biggest, baddest lawman in all of Wyoming," boasted one man holding a gun to Slocum's head. "And he's done run you to ground.

Now answer him, you son of a bitch." The man kicked Slocum hard in the ribs.

Slocum grunted and doubled up, his scratched, bloodied arms coming in to his body to clutch his chest.

"Hold it!" snapped the deputy marshal, seeing how Slocum reacted. "Reach for that Colt of yours and we kill you here and now instead of letting you stand trial."

"Let me shoot him, Billy," begged the man who had kicked Slocum. "You owe me."

"I don't owe you squat. You wouldn't even be here if you weren't my brother-in-law."

"Ah, Billy," the man said.

"Address me as Deputy Gaines," the lawman grated out. He came around, flipped Slocum's ebony-handled Colt Navy from its holster and hefted it. "You use this a powerful lot. This is a gunfighter's sidearm and its mighty worn. Now, tell me where the rest of the rustlers are or I might just plug you with your own gun." The deputy aimed Slocum's own six-shooter at him.

"I was tracking the rustlers to turn them over to the cavalry," Slocum said, sitting up. His ribs ached but didn't hurt too bad. Nothing had been broken by the savage kick.

"Yeah, and I'm President Grant," the deputy snapped. "We want the whole sorry lot of you. Where'd they get off to? And where'd they take the cattle you've been stealin' for the past two months?"

"That was a slick trick you pulled, sendin' us on a wild goose chase over to the Mountain View railhead, too," spoke up Gaines's in-law.

"Shut up," Gaines said without rancor. His reply to his brother-in-law sounded automatic, as if he was so accustomed to it that he didn't have to think about it anymore.

"I'm the foreman at the Triple Cross," Slocum said, sucking in air and fighting down the moment of giddiness from the pain. But he was sure no ribs had been broken.

"Sure you are," Gaines said. "Chafee's the foreman,

and I've known him for half my life." To his posse, the deputy marshal said, "Get him on his feet and hog-tie him good. We'll take him back to Kemmerer for trial."

"Ask Mr. Mathiesen," Slocum said. "He made me foreman after Chafee was gunned down."

"A likely story. What'd you do, hear Chafee's name mentioned in some saloon? I didn't fall off the turnip truck this morning." Gaines gestured impatiently and his men roughly shoved Slocum around.

"You want us to go back to hidin', Billy?"

"No one's comin' back," Gaines said angrily. "We got to be satisfied with grabbin' one of them owlhoots. But where'd they go with the beeves? There's quite a reward for gettin' a herd that size back."

Gaines and his brother-in-law walked away, arguing while two others trussed Slocum up and then heaved him belly-down over his saddle. The ride to Kemmerer was pure torture for him, and being locked in the iron cage was almost a relief.

Almost.

Slocum had argued with the deputy marshal about sending word to the Triple Cross to verify his identity, but Gaines refused. He claimed he needed the posse all together to hunt for the main body of rustlers and to find the cattle they'd stolen. As much as Slocum understood that this was reasonable, it still rankled. He was no rustler and he wanted out of the Kemmerer prison.

From what he could tell of the small town, it wasn't much larger than Fort Bridger but had the distinction of a fair-sized jailhouse and a federal deputy marshal entrusted with keeping the peace in all of southwestern Wyoming.

Slocum paced about the small cell, looking at the rivets and thick straps holding him so securely. He had dug down a few inches in the dirt floor, only to find he was surrounded by the iron. No way to tunnel out, no way to break free. All he could do was sit and wait for the circuit judge and a trial that would undoubtedly find him guilty. The verdict wasn't something Slocum looked forward to hearing.

He had to get out of jail before then. How he was going to do it was something he had not figured out. Yet.

Sinking to the cot, he stared past the bars to the deputy's desk fifteen feet away. Even if Gaines left the keys where he could see them, Slocum had no way of reaching that far.

He perked up when the outer door opened and two people came in to speak with the deputy marshal.

"Good day, sir," said Othniel Marsh. "It is my understanding that you have a prisoner incarcerated here."

"I've got a cattle rustler locked up in the back, if that's what you mean."

Marsh and the deputy exchanged more words, but Slocum's eyes were fixed on Ella Weedin. She waved to him and smiled her mischievous smile. For the first time in a week, Slocum dared hope he might get out of the Kemmerer jail.

"You're not pullin' my leg, now, are you? I kin toss you in the cell next to his if you're lyin' to me," the deputy marshal said hotly.

"Sir, my card. Please send a telegram to the curator of the Peabody Museum, Yale University, if you need to verify my identity. I am Othniel Marsh, Professor of Antiquities, and quite highly respected in my field, I might add."

"Oh, come now, Marshal," Ella said sweetly when she saw Gaines wasn't impressed by Marsh's credentials, "why would we lie to you?"

Her charms bounced off Billy Gaines's thick hide as fast as Marsh's claim to academic notoriety. If anything Ella made him more suspicious.

"He claims he works for a spread down south," Gaines said.

"After poor Mr. Chafee was killed, John took over as foreman of the Triple Cross," Ella said.

Slocum wondered how she had known that. She or Marsh must have stopped by the ranch to talk to Mathiesen, possibly to urge the old drover to release Slocum for more important work: digging up bones.

"So Chafee's really dead?" asked Gaines. "Damned shame. He was a good man."

"The rustlers you apparently seek in all the wrong places were responsible for Mr. Chafee's demise," Marsh said. "Or so Mr. Mathiesen, a most charming old gentleman, informed us."

"Slocum's not one of the rustlers?" asked Gaines, sounding disappointed. "I got the judge comin' around in a couple weeks. I don't want his trip to be for nuthin'."

"We assure you Mr. Slocum is a decent, hardworking man." The way Ella emphasized the syllable "hard" made Slocum wince. The deputy didn't notice anything.

"I can't up and let him go, not without a hearing. I might have the wrong galoot, but that's up for the court to decide."

"You would consider bail?" asked Marsh, digging in his coat pocket and drawing out a wallet crammed with greenbacks. "Or perhaps payment of a fine for, oh, disturbing the peace? Or a few dollars to recompense you for the time Mr. Slocum has spent eating your food and dwelling under the roof of this, uh, fine establishment?"

"A hunnerd dollars and your personal guarantee that he don't cause no trouble. If he does, I swear I won't rest till I track him down."

"I'll be sure Mr. Slocum behaves properly," Ella assured him sweetly. "Do pay the lawman, Professor."

Money changed hands, and Slocum was let out of the cage. The deputy watched him go with growing suspicion, as if he were unsure he was doing the right thing.

"I'm keepin' your six-shooter till you leave Kemmerer," Gaines said. "That'll guarantee you don't go gettin' in any more trouble."

"I—" Slocum started to protest, but Ella silenced him.

"For the foreseeable future, we'll be in the barn outside town," Professor Marsh said.

"You the gent what rented that fallin' down relic?" asked Gaines. He laughed. "You better repair the roof 'fore you put any horses in those stalls. Otherwise, your stock'll get pneumonia after the first good rain."

"Oh, fear not, my good man," Marsh said condescendingly. "The animals I have placed within the structure are not prone to disease. They are long gone."

"What?"

"I intend to have a public showing in another day or so. You may satisfy your curiosity then," said Marsh.

"You don't go nowhere, Slocum. You stay in Kemmerer, hear, boy?"

Slocum didn't trust himself to speak. He had taken a real dislike to the deputy marshal, but the desire to see the sun again was stronger than his need to bandy words.

He stepped into the street and got his first good view of the town. A week earlier, they had arrived in Kemmerer after dark. Being folded belly-down over his saddle hadn't given Slocum much of an opportunity to look around, either.

"I'm sorry we didn't hear of the deputy's prisoner sooner, John," said Ella. "Even when I did hear, it never occurred to me that that foolish badge-wearing bumpkin had locked *you* up."

"Thanks for getting me out," Slocum said. He looked around, wondering if he could find his Appaloosa and ride out before the deputy knew he was gone. He would owe Marsh a hundred dollars if he skipped bail, but then he had not asked the professor to put up his own money.

"We can use some help at our exhibit," Marsh said briskly, coming from the deputy's office. "Go see to our supplies at the general store, Mr. Slocum."

Slocum bristled at being ordered about like a menial. Ella put a gentling hand on his arm to keep him from saying or doing anything he might regret. From the corner of his eye, Slocum saw the deputy marshal watching them like hawks.

"All right," he said, resolved to making the best of the situation. "Where's this barn?"

"I'll go with you, John," Ella volunteered.

"No, my dear, you need to finish the drawings. They are an integral part of the display."

"I can find the place," Slocum said. He doubted it could be too hard to find the recently abandoned barn where a crazy man put up skeletons of strange, huge animals. Everyone in Kemmerer would be talking about it, though he had hoped Ella would be free to show him around. They could have spent a few pleasurable hours getting the supplies. Slocum felt he deserved some kind of reward for rotting in the deputy's jail for a full week, and Ella was the person to deliver that compensation.

The professor and Ella hurried off to the north end of town. Slocum got his bearings, then headed south, looking for the general store and Marsh's supplies. He spotted the large store at the intersection of the two main streets and cut kitty-corner to reach it. He was almost run down by a man whipping his horse furiously to a gallop.

"Watch it!" Slocum called, jumping out of the way as the horse and carriage raced past. The driver stopped his punishment of the horse and brought the rig to a halt. He jumped out and stormed back to confront Slocum in the middle of the street.

"You stole my most valuable find! You're a thief!" shouted Edward Cope. "You robbed me!"

"Whoa, hold on," Slocum said. He reached down but

found only an empty holster. Gaines hadn't given him back his Colt Navy. "You're creating quite a stir." He looked around at the crowd gathering and knew it was only a matter of minutes before the deputy came running to find out what had caused the disturbance.

"You and the hussy, that . . . that fallen woman!" raged Cope, almost incoherent now. "The pair of you stole my compsognathnus! My finest specimen!"

"What are you goin' on about, mister?" asked Deputy Marshal Gaines, finally arriving.

"This thief! He stole a theropod from me."

"What'n the bloody hell's that?" asked Gaines, resting his hand on his holstered six-shooter, ready to throw down on Slocum if he tried to make a run for it. Slocum wasn't moving a muscle.

"It's a small dinosaur, possibly a type of bird," Cope said, still sputtering. By now half the town had gathered to watch.

"He ain't got no bird on him. I just let him out of jail," Gaines said. "And he didn't have a bird in his larder when I arrested him, either."

"You had him in jail and you let him go? He's a thief! He and Marsh. They're crooks. And that woman's even worse." Cope rattled on, but Slocum caught Gaines's eye and drew the deputy to one side.

"He might have been out in the sun a mite too long," Slocum suggested.

"You couldn't have stolen anything. I've had you locked up, and I never set eyes on him before a day or two ago." Gaines frowned, trying to figure out what to do. Slocum knew the lawman wanted to start throwing people into his jail, since it was so achingly empty at the moment, but he refrained.

"This here's a cowboy, mister. What else he might be I don't have much idea, but I've got my eye on him. But if you want to swear out a complaint, I kin take it over at my office."

"You let him go once. You'd do it again," said Cope. "I'll see justice done. Mark my words!"

"No gunplay in this town," Gaines warned sternly. "I'll heave your scrawny butt into jail so fast if you try to shoot it out, your head won't stop spinnin' for a month of Sundays."

Cope sputtered some more, then whirled and stormed away.

"You've still got my six-gun, Deputy," Slocum pointed out.

"It's gonna stay in my desk, under lock and key, too. I don't think you got much to worry about from him, 'less he tries to talk you to death."

Slocum knew he could handle Cope, if it came to that. Somehow, he thought the paleontologist was all bluster and no bite.

"He's a strange fella," Gaines went on. "Not that Marsh ain't a tad peculiar, too." Gaines looked at Slocum with something approaching pity and then hitched up his gunbelt and went on his way.

Slocum saw the crowd that had gathered slowly disappear, going about their business. He made his way through the horses and wagons and went to the store, where he found a pile of sacks with Marsh's name scrawled on them in paint.

"These all go to the professor?" Slocum asked when a man approaching emaciation came out and peered at him through thick glasses.

"Reckon so. That's his name I wrote. You his hired help?"

Slocum bristled at the notion he was Marsh's menial, but he only nodded. As soon as he got his six-shooter back, he would be on his way out of Kemmerer.

"He said for you to use my wagon. Paid good for the

rental, too," the store owner said. "It's out back. Team's all hitched up and ready to roll."

Slocum spent the next half hour loading the sacks into the wagon bed, wondering what Marsh wanted with so much plaster of Paris. The best he could tell, that's all any of the bags held. With this much plaster, Othniel Marsh could build himself a house and finish off all the inside walls. Slocum doubted this was what the professor intended, though.

He got the wagon moving and drove to the north side of town. As Marsh had said, it was hard to miss the tumbledown barn. Red paint had peeled off, exposing the wood to the elements. Wind and sun and worms had destroyed many of the planks that had once formed the sides. Slocum remembered what the deputy marshal had said about the roof.

It probably leaked like a sieve.

"John, John! Come on inside and see what the professor has done." Ella waved to him.

"Where's he want the plaster? I'll take care of unloading first."

"Oh, pish. Forget that for right now. Come see his handiwork. The man is a true genius." Ella's insistence forced Slocum to go into the barn and see the strangest sight he could remember witnessing.

Stretching the entire length of the barn towered a skeleton, easily fifteen feet tall. The size of its rib cage was intimidating, but not as intimidating as the huge head with jaws around teeth bigger than Bowie knives.

Slocum couldn't help but stare in wonder at the huge skeleton.

12

"It's an allosaurus. Or an excellent replica of one." Ella sounded downright proud. Slocum wasn't sure what she meant until he walked over and touched a part of the monster's tail.

"Those aren't real bones," Slocum said, examining the creation closer. White dust came off on his fingers after he rubbed the vertebra. "It's made from plaster."

"Why, of course it is. Plaster is much lighter and easier to wire together. Professor Marsh makes a cast from the real bone, carefully splits it, removes the real fossil, then fills the cast with plaster and *voila*! A dinosaur for display. He followed my sketches exactly, making the assembly that much easier."

Slocum's hand involuntarily moved to his empty holster, then realized that not only did Deputy Gaines still have his six-shooter, but no pistol was going to bring down the threat posed by such a huge beast if it had attacked him in the flesh.

"Is this real? Was it?" Slocum asked, not sure how to phrase his question. He stared at the colossal creature, unable to believe it had ever existed.

"Oh, quite real, yes, quite real. But now, more's the

pity, this fellow is decidedly extinct," said Othniel Marsh, coming in from the rear of the barn. "Extinct means it no longer walks the earth, but it did once."

"When?" asked Slocum.

"I am not certain to any degree of precision, but at least ten million years ago. Perhaps longer. Professor Mudge at Yale thinks it might date to fifty million years ago, though I think that is extreme in light of Sir Charles Lyell's work on geologic aging."

"I'd want a big rifle to bring this one down," Slocum said. He wondered if even a .60-caliber buffalo rifle would be powerful enough to stop a creature like this if it came charging at him across the prairie. More than the size of the gun, it would take a hunter with quite a lot of sand in his gizzard to keep from running if faced with such a monster. "How much meat could you dress out from it?"

Marsh laughed. "Perhaps several tons, but it was a predator and might not be too tasty."

"I've got more plaster of Paris outside," Slocum said, shaking himself free from the spell cast by this behemoth dinosaur. He had a hard time believing the plaster carcass represented anything that had ever walked the Wyoming grasslands.

"Excellent, yes, come along and I'll show you where to store it. I intend to cast several more of these beasts and charge the good people of Kemmerer fifty cents to witness that which stalked their land in bygone days. I am perfecting my techniques here so that I might be utterly expert when I return to Yale."

Slocum nodded. This was something he understood. He had seen P. T. Barnum's travelling show a few years back and doubted any of the freaks and monstrosities on display were real, but they made for good entertainment. Slocum had to think Marsh's dinosaur fell into the same class.

Slocum, Ella and Marsh went to the wagon, but the

professor quickly left when he saw all was proceeding according to plan. Several of Marsh's crew were already unloading the heavy sacks. Slocum pitched in to help, and as the last of the bags was stored in a building some ways behind the barn, he paused and cocked his head to one side.

"What's wrong, John?" asked Ella. "You look as if someone's walking on your grave."

"There's something wrong," he said. Again his hand went for the empty holster. "Did Marsh post guards on his plaster dinosaur? I thought I heard something moving around in the barn."

"Why, no, I don't think he left anyone inside. Except the dinosaur. You don't think Big Al's come alive, do you?" Ella laughed. The sound was like silver bells in a soft spring wind.

"Big Al?"

"My name for the allosaurus. Oh, look, the professor's back."

Slocum saw Marsh at the front of a crowd of townspeople, looking for all the world like the Pied Piper.

"Come one, come all, see the scientific discovery of the century!" bellowed Marsh, as any carnival barker might harangue his marks. The professor motioned, and his men worked their way through the crowd, selling tickets to the display for fifty cents. Slocum tried to keep count. Marsh had to be close to a hundred dollars ahead by the time the first of the gawkers went into the barn.

Marsh had entered with them to begin his spiel, but an outraged cry from the professor brought Slocum around. He dashed to the barn door, pushing aside the paying patrons. Ella crowded in behind him.

"Who ruined it? My beautiful allosaurus is ruined! Look at that!" moaned Marsh.

Slocum laughed at the sight of the head placed inside the rib cage, the long neck craned about through an impossible arc. It looked as if the creature had rammed its knife-toothed head up its rear end.

Slocum backed from the barn and cast around for the culprit who had rearranged the bones in such a vulgar fashion. He didn't have to look long at the crowd before he spotted Edward Cope, a fierce grin on his face.

"What's goin' on?" Deputy Gaines pushed through the throng to the sputtering Othniel Marsh.

Slocum saw his chance and took it. While the deputy marshal was occupied listening to Marsh's tale of academic sabotage, Slocum made his way back down Kemmerer's main street and quickly entered the jailhouse. Stealing behind the deputy's desk, he tried the desk drawers and finally jiggled the center one open. There lay his Colt Navy.

Slocum hastily returned it to its usual place and felt fully dressed for the first time since the deputy had captured him. It was time to hightail it now. Marsh had paid off the deputy marshal, and Gaines had said reluctantly that Slocum was probably not a rustler. The only one who would have any complaint if Slocum left Kemmerer might be Marsh, since he had posted the bail money.

If so, Slocum knew the professor would get over it eventually.

As he stepped from the jail he saw Ella Weedin at the far end of the street. She smiled and waved cheerily to him. Then she turned to slow the deputy's return to his office.

Slocum slipped around the jailhouse and found his Appaloosa with his gear at the livery stable. He rode from town, the feeling in his gut that he was likely to see both Ella and the deputy marshal again.

Slocum half-listened to Tatum's recitation of everything that had gone wrong on the Triple Cross Ranch in his absence. Slocum had thought settling back down into the job of foreman might give him time to catch his breath. Far from it.

"So we got a couple cases of dynamite to blow them stumps. You know the ones I mean, don't you, Mr. Slocum?"

"Yeah, the ones to the north, the place where Mathiesen wants to raise some hay to help weather the herd."

"That's the place. Real rocky, too. Dynamite's gonna be good for blowin' up them rocks."

"What about the cattle? Are you sure we've lost another ten head?"

"As sure as my name's Jesse Tatum," the young man declared solemnly. "Fallon and me both worked the range and found a few calves without their mamas."

"Wolves," Slocum said, knowing it wasn't likely. Tatum might be inexperienced, but the evidence of a predator attack would have been obvious to any greenhorn.

"No carcasses. Never heard of a wolf pack or a coyote draggin' off the skeleton and all."

"Did you notify the cavalry over at the fort?"

"Didn't do no good. They brushed me off, but I passed along Mr. Mathiesen's worry on the matter. They're not doin' a heck of a lot to catch the rustlers, are they?"

"What's eating you?" Slocum asked.

"I don't think it was the rustlers that got the beeves. Not this time. Oh, I mean it was rustlers, but not the same ones."

"Arapahos?" guessed Slocum. Tatum's eyes widened in surprise.

"Mr. Slocum, you are amazing. Did you do one of them mind reading things?"

"If it's not wolves or the gang of rustlers—and they might be hightailing it out of the territory since the deputy marshal up in Kemmerer is bound and determined to catch them—who's left?"

"Well, you did take care of them fellows digging up

the bones who was shootin' our cows," said Tatum, face screwed up in thought. "Reckon I see how you guessed."

Slocum grumbled a mite under his breath. He was feeling more and more boxed in. Wyoming had not been his destination when he left St. Louis, and the Pacific Coast called to him louder by the day. But he owed Mr. Mathiesen a smoothly running spread before moving on, and Chafee's killers hadn't been brought to justice yet. Slocum's unfinished business held him as surely as chains could, and he didn't much like that.

"I'll see what I can do to talk with the Arapahos," Slocum said. "I know where their camp is."

"That's downright dangerous, Mr. Slocum. What if they scalp you?"

"Then they'll have my hairpiece to go along with a supper of some mighty find Triple Cross steak," Slocum said. Tatum looked shocked, but Slocum's laugh put the young man at ease. "You get out there and mark the stumps that have to be removed and any rocks that can be turned into gravel. I'll be back before you know it."

Slocum had hoped to rest a day or two before getting into the saddle again, but it hadn't worked that way for him. Tatum had brought the problem of the missing cattle to him within minutes of his boot touching ground after his long, tiring ride south from Kemmerer. Still, Slocum was grateful to be out of the jail and riding under the burning summer sun. The wind gusted past his face, and the scent of things growing all around him restored his good humor as much as anything could.

He was free here, no matter how tied down he felt working as the Triple Cross Ranch's foreman.

Tatum had given him an idea where the cattle had gone missing, but Slocum veered from that part of the ranch and headed to the bone yard he had shown Ella. It didn't surprise him to find four of Marsh's men hard at work digging in the center of the Arapahos' sacred ground. He never bothered to talk to the workers, since he knew they would never stop unless ordered to do so by Othniel Marsh.

Or if he killed them. Slocum toyed with that idea, then knew Marsh would only send more. Better to deal directly with him and convince him of the danger.

The men standing guard with their rifles at ready also deterred him. He wasn't inclined to start a major fight he couldn't win.

Circling the bone field, leaving the paleontologists to their work, Slocum found a trail made by a half dozen cattle and at least that many riders, on unshod horses. Slocum got to what he thought was the far side of the Indian burial ground and then stopped for the night.

A small fire burned fitfully, the green wood snapping and sizzling as it heated sap to the boiling point. Slocum fixed himself coffee and a plate of beans. He still had a can of peaches, but he saved that for breakfast. All his bacon had turned so rancid he could not bear the thought of eating it, even if he was starving to death.

As he sat and poked at the fire, occasionally taking a sip of his coffee, Slocum felt a presence. He continued to pay no attention to his feelings, even when a dark figure loomed on the far side of his fire.

For several minutes, Slocum ignored the Arapaho as the brave stood silently. Finally, Slocum looked up and said, "Want some coffee? It's not the best, but I'd be proud to share it with you."

The Arapaho stepped forward. Slocum held down his surprise when he saw this wasn't just any hunter, but a chief. Burning Knife's reputation as a war chief was great and honestly earned.

"You can sit," Slocum said, pointing to a rock opposite him on the other side of the fire. The way the hair on the back of his neck stood up, Slocum knew Burning Knife had not come alone. He might have a hundred warriors out in the darkness waiting to fill Slocum with arrows and bullets.

"You share?"

"I am honored by such a famous chief's presence in my camp," Slocum said. Slocum poured coffee into his cup and passed it over, while pouring more for himself in the shallow lid to the coffeepot and then sipping at it. He never bothered carrying two tin cups when he was on the trail, and this was the best he could do to show hospitality.

Burning Knife nodded once, acknowledging that he was such a man. They sat quietly, drinking coffee for several more minutes, until Burning Knife said, "They dig up our land."

"You steal another man's cattle," Slocum replied, knowing such boldness might be his death. His hand was steady as he poured more coffee and looked squarely into the Arapaho chief's eyes. This rudeness angered Burning Knife.

"They dig sacred ground! If they do not stop, we kill them!"

"Why haven't you done that already?" Slocum asked. "You're a fierce war chief." He thought he knew the answer, but he wanted to force Burning Knife to admit that his band of warriors was small. Perhaps the cavalry had hounded them until they were starving and unable to make a stand. If Burning Knife was caught, he would undoubtedly be sent back to the reservation—or possibly hanged.

The former might be a worse fate for a proud warrior. Slocum understood that. For all the service he had gotten from the cavalry post at Fort Bridger, Slocum found himself siding more with the Arapahos in their quest to stay free of the reservation.

"We do not go onto sacred ground to kill white-eyes," Burning Knife said. "Our spirits would forever walk this world and be kept from the Happy Hunting Grounds."

Slocum nodded. This was possible, too. He suspected

Burning Knife didn't have the braves to fight Marsh's party, small as it was.

"It is a great honor to meet a chief of your courage. I give you many gifts."

"Gifts?" This perked up Burning Knife.

"You may keep all the cattle you have taken. Consider this a gift from Mathiesen, the great chief of the white-eyes."

"We have the cows already!"

"Take any more and the great chief Mathiesen will kill you, your warriors and your women and children. He will steal your horses and shoot your dogs."

This caused Burning Knife to ponder the situation for several minutes.

"I accept the gift of great chief Mathiesen."

"You are as wise as you are brave," Slocum said.

"Do those who destroy our sacred ground ride under the totem of the great chief Mathiesen?"

"No," Slocum said.

"We will kill them when they leave."

"Do so and more white-eyes will come. Many, many more. And the cavalry, too, with their big guns," Slocum said, knowing how this would affect the Arapaho if he was truly on the run from the bluecoats. "Let me talk to those who dig on your sacred grounds. If they leave after I talk to them, they will not return."

"And others?"

"No others will come. The land will remain sacred to the Arapaho."

Burning Knife nodded once, finished his coffee and stood abruptly, throwing the tin cup to the ground. Without another word, he turned and vanished into the night. Slocum reached over and picked up the discarded cup, sloshed around a little coffee and then poured himself what remained in the pot.

Burning Knife was capable of attacking Marsh's men

as they tried to get the dinosaur bones out of the burial ground, but Slocum thought the Arapahos were more inclined to move on than to wait. Let them keep the stolen cattle if that meant they would drive the beeves back to their village to feed the squaws, children and old men.

But if he couldn't get Marsh's men to leave once and for all, Burning Knife was likely to come back—and not just to steal cattle.

13

"Sorry, Mr. Slocum. I don't know what coulda happened
to it," said Tatum, scratching his head. "I left it out, so
it's my fault. Never in a hunnerd years did I think anybody'd steal it."

"You're sure someone took the case of dynamite?"
asked Slocum. He felt as if a ton of rocks weighed him
down. For every minor problem on the Triple Cross he
solved, two more cropped up. The past couple days, since
he had returned from parleying with Burning Knife and
threatening Othniel Marsh with enough violence to force
him out of the Arapaho burial grounds, had been quiet
enough, dealing with routine, but he worried that the gang
of rustlers would start stealing cattle again. Something had
to be done about finding them and stopping the preda-
tions. But he had never thought theft of a case of dynamite
would be a more immediate worry.

"I scouted around, like I seen you do. Got down on my
hands and knees and found tracks in the dirt. Real faint.
Couldn't make out more'n one or two of 'em, but they
was heavier leavin' the place where I stashed the dynamite
than they was comin'."

Slocum ignored Tatum's guesswork. A case of dyna-

116

mite wouldn't weigh enough to cause a noticeable difference in the imprint when a man carried it. This was especially hard to judge if the land was rocky or even grassy, as was most of the area where Tatum had gone to blast stumps and large rocks.

"The entire case is gone?"

"It didn't up and waltz away on its own," Tatum said.

Slocum doubted the young man had a lying bone in his body. Fallon he didn't much trust, but he figured Fallon was better than Longmeadow ever had been when it came to loyalty to the Triple Cross. The cowboys still working for Mathiesen might have their faults, but they weren't working both sides against the middle. They took their pay and were happy for it and Mrs. Mathiesen's cooking.

"The only people in the area who'd steal something like that are the two bone hunting expeditions," Slocum said, thinking aloud. "Either Marsh or Cope is capable of stealing a case of dynamite. I don't think an Arapaho would take it."

"Them rustlers might," Tatum said, "but for the life of me I don't know why."

"Men like that steal for the pleasure they get out of it," Slocum said, but he agreed. Rustlers had little use for a crate of explosives. If he had to bet, he would put his entire stake on one of the two paleontologists.

"What do you reckon we ought to do about it, Mr. Slocum?"

"Nothing," he decided. "Mr. Mathiesen's out the cost of the dynamite. That doesn't equal even the loss of one steer. We keep our eyes open for rustlers and go into town and get another case of dynamite."

"That's logical," Tatum said, smiling as he worked through what Slocum had said. "I sure am learnin' a lot from you, Mr. Slocum."

Slocum didn't like the role of being a teacher, but most of the ranch hands were as wet behind the ears as Tatum and needed someone helping them figure out the right way to do things. The best he could tell, Tatum had been raised in Kansas City, and the closest he had ever been to a cow as a child was watching trains laden with the beeves head northward to Chicago. Something had put the bug in his ear to come west and he had, with the clothes on his back and little else—and that lack included knowledge of earning his keep.

Prying into the young man's past wasn't something Slocum would ever do. Tatum's parents might have thrown him out or they might have died. Or it could be the man simply got the wanderlust and lit out on his own. As long as he put in a day's work for his pay, Slocum was content not to nose around in another man's business.

"Why don't you take three or four of the hands and go scour the area, in case the dynamite got misplaced."

"All right." Tatum hesitated, then grinned broadly. "You sayin' I'm in charge?"

"I need someone to work as my right-hand man. You're as good as any of the others. Learn enough and I'll ask Mr. Mathiesen to make you foreman when I move on."

"I hope that's not for a spell, Mr. Slocum."

Slocum wasn't sure when it might be. Sooner rather than later felt right, but he had business to tend to before considering it. And he didn't mean herding. Nobody had done anything to find Chafee's killer, and Deputy Marshal Billy Gaines might be warming a chair back in Kemmerer rather than hunting for the elusive cattle rustlers. Slocum hadn't heard any rumors of the lawman actively tracking the outlaws.

Slocum had Chafee's murderer to run down, along with the rest of the gang of rustlers, and now the thief who had swiped a case of dynamite was added to his list. In spite of what Slocum told Tatum about it not being important, somebody had a definite use for that much explosive. Slocum wanted to get it back before he found out how much damage could be done with fifty-percent sticks of dynamite.

As he had told Tatum, first things came first: find the rustlers.

The Triple Cross was in good enough hands having Tatum look after the herd and the day-to-day chores. Calving was long past, and most of them were old enough to have been branded. The summer months mostly were spent keeping the cattle from straying too far across the wide-open Wyoming grasslands and getting them fat for the autumn drive to the railhead. It was a good time for Tatum to learn by experience what he didn't already know from Slocum telling him.

Mostly, it let Slocum take a few days to hunt for the gang of rustlers. He wanted to run them to earth before they preyed even more on the Triple Cross herd, but Slocum also had another reason for sweeping through the countryside. He wanted to find the dynamite. He worried more about its loss than he had let on to Tatum. If they had been closer to a big town, Slocum knew the dynamite could have been put to good use blowing open a bank safe. From what he had seen of Fort Bridger, all that was needed to rob any of the businesses there was a little determination and a leveled six-shooter.

Dynamite blew things up. Slocum wanted to find out the target before it erupted in his face. More than this, though, he wanted to find the damned rustlers.

On his second day out sweeping across the prairie, Slocum came across a butchered steer. Traces around the animal carcass showed that another four or five beeves had been driven off. He had found the rustlers' trail, and this time he wasn't going to let them give him the slip. Slocum smiled ruefully, wondering if the deputy marshal was also hunting the outlaws. If so, Slocum wanted to avoid being tarred with the same brush again.

The tracks went arrow-straight toward hills that were all too familiar to Slocum. He had come this way enough times before to know the landmarks along the trail. As he rode toward Marsh's camp, intending to look in on Ella as much as anything else, the ground shook hard. His Appaloosa reared and forced Slocum to concentrate for several seconds on gentling the horse. When no second shock came, he knew he had found the dynamite—or part of the stolen crate.

Slocum found himself torn between continuing after the outlaws and the cattle they had stolen or going to see if anyone had been hurt in the explosion. At least, he had the answer to the dynamite thief's identity. Othniel Marsh would have to pay for that, too.

If he already hadn't by having the explosive blow him to Kingdom Come.

Slocum made his decision. He took as good a sighting on the rustlers' trail as he could, fixed the landmarks in his head and then trotted in the direction of the professor's camp. When he was still a half mile away he saw the dust cloud still billowing upward into the air. To cause such a fuss, at least four sticks had to have been detonated.

He picked up the pace and got to the professor's camp in time to see two men dragging a third toward a tent. In spite of his bloodied condition, Slocum recognized the injured man as Sanborn, Marsh's foreman on the dig.

"You turn up at the oddest of times, Mr. Slocum," Othniel Marsh said, coming over. The professor's face was streaked with blood and dust and he limped. His pant leg had been shredded, and what was left of the cloth hung in tatters.

"Anything I can do?" Slocum asked, looking around for Ella. There was no reason for her to have been in the pit where the explosion had occurred—unless she had been sketching the bones.

"The genie is out of the bottle, so to speak," Marsh

said. "I'm not sure what happened or if there is any way for you to fix it. Poor Sanborn seems to have had his head rattled about."

"Why did you steal the dynamite?" Slocum asked bluntly. Marsh blinked, and Slocum could almost believe the scientist knew nothing about it.

"I told Sanborn to hurry along with the excavation, especially since there are such fine fields to explore elsewhere." Marsh looked up at Slocum, a defiant look on his face. Slocum knew the man meant the bone field in the middle of the Arapahos' burial ground, but he didn't call him on it. The professor had left the field with ill grace, but Slocum's vivid descriptions of what the Indians would do had convinced him. "I told him to proceed faster, but he knows better than to use dynamite. Any such explosion might shatter the fragile skeletons we work so hard to remove."

Slocum saw that Marsh was still dazed from the explosion.

"Mind if I look around? There might be some unexploded dynamite left."

Marsh made a vague gesture with his hand and wandered off. Slocum considered getting some of the others in the expedition to look after him, then decided locating the rest of the dynamite was more important. Shock would wear off. If another worker chanced on the dynamite left in the stolen crate and somehow detonated it, there would be pieces flying all over the site.

Slocum went to the edge of the excavation, surprised at the extent now. When he had visited before, the plains had been dug up several feet down over a wide area. Now the hole went almost fifteen feet into the ground, as if Marsh were closing in on some particular set of bones. The square pit was still close to twenty feet on a side, but ladders were necessary to get to the floor.

Of the three ladders, only one remained. The other two had been blown to splinters.

Seeing that caused Slocum to wonder if Cope might not be escalating the battle and have taken to outright murder. A big enough charge would have killed the men in the pit and possibly caused the sides to cave in, providing a handy grave for the dead.

"Old bones and new," Slocum muttered as he went to the ladder, swung about and quickly descended. The explosion had caused considerable damage to the dinosaur skeleton still embedded in the rocky floor. The chalky white was spotted with bright red drops of drying blood everywhere he looked.

Walking about slowly, Slocum got a better idea of what had happened. Marsh was right. Sanborn wasn't responsible for using the dynamite, if he had been working in the pit. The blast had chewed a tiny crater five feet to one side, about where a parcel of four sticks would have been tossed from the surface, eight feet above.

Someone had tried to kill the workmen. Or perhaps the intent was to close the pit. Either way, Marsh was lucky none of his laborers had died.

Slocum had spent some time as a hard rock miner and knew about supporting walls and mine shafts. He examined the pit walls and decided the blast had not seriously damaged them to the point they had to be reinforced before further work on the dinosaur bones could continue.

He climbed back up the ladder and circled the mouth of the pit to the place where he thought someone had dropped in the deadly bomb. He found a spent lucifer and a blasting cap that had been crimped in someone's teeth but had not held the fuse properly.

Slocum reenacted the attempt to stop Marsh's digging. A man had walked over, taken out a blasting cap and a few inches of miner's fuse, tried to crimp the first cap and failed. He had spat it out, then used a second, putting cap and fuse into the center of the dynamite sticks. A match came out, lit the fuse, the bomber walked to the edge of the pit, tossed it in and then . . . ran.

The would be killer's stride to the pit had been deliberate. Going away, he was running for his life since he didn't want to be anywhere near the pit if it caved in from the blast.

Slocum followed the boot prints to a spot in a stand of junipers where a horse had been hidden.

"Othniel said you were nosing about, John," came Ella's soft voice.

"What have you found?"

The auburn-haired artist looked frazzled but as beautiful as ever. Minor blood smears on her sleeves and down the front of her once crisp white blouse showed she had been acting as nurse but had not been injured herself.

"Somebody wants to get rid of your expedition," Slocum said.

"Cope," she said, but in a voice lacking her usual venom when speaking of Marsh's rival. "Who else?"

Slocum ignored the question. He was beginning to believe that he had been wrong concerning the identity of the dynamite thief. The rustlers were more likely suspects by the minute, though why they would want to chase off Marsh's expedition was something he had yet to answer.

"How's Sanborn?"

"He'll be all right. He's got a broken arm and more rock shards in him than that morosaurus—it's a huge sauropod," she said, seeing he didn't understand. "There's quite a fight going on over the skeleton," she went on. "Cope claims it is only another specimen of the camarsaurus that he discovered. Marsh is sure—"

"It doesn't matter," Slocum said, interrupting here. He did not understand these people. Piles of bones meant more to them than blowing up one another.

"Sanborn will be fine," Ella said. "Who'd have thought you cared."

"If he was dead, you'd have to let the deputy marshal up in Kemmerer know."

"Billy Gaines? That man's a buffoon," she said.

"The federal deputy marshal buffoon," Slocum corrected. "As it stands, there's no reason to let him know what happened." Slocum hesitated, then asked, "Where are Marsh's guards? I didn't see them when I rode up, and they certainly did nothing to stop someone dropping a bomb on Sanborn's head."

"They, well, it's like this, John. Marsh is running very close to the limits of his budget and had to let them go, the ones that didn't quit outright after you chased us away from the Arapaho burial ground site. Maybe Marsh shouldn't have let the remaining guards go, but it came down to using fewer workmen or dismissing the guards."

"Tell him to keep at least one guard on lookout. This might happen again. There's still most of a case of dynamite missing from the Triple Cross." He turned from her, but she caught his arm and held it.

"Do you have to go? Right away? Stay for supper, at least. I'm certain the professor will want to talk to you as soon as his shock wears off."

He stared into her limpid blue eyes and almost agreed. Then he remembered he had rustlers—murderers and would-be murderers—to track down. The owlhoots were growing bolder, no longer content simply to steal cattle, and had to be stopped right away. He had seen this same behavior when a wolf turned vicious. A small bloody victory fed its appetite for more, until it was crazed enough to take on a grizzly or black bear. The bear could usually finish even the most berserk wolf, but the animals killed getting to that point were what concerned Slocum.

The rustlers would work their way through the cowboys on the Triple Cross, the workers at Marsh's site and maybe even Cope's, enjoying the sensation of another's death.

Slocum intended to be the grizzly that put a stop to their death spree.

"I see you're going after whoever did this. Thank you, John. And when you come back, I'll see you get a proper payment." For the first time, the pixie smile fluttered across her lips and her azure eyes sparkled. Then the shock and fatigue returned.

"Keep a sharp watch," Slocum said. He bent, kissed her lightly and then forced himself away reluctantly to retrieve his Appaloosa from behind Marsh's tent, where it had been greedily drinking from the small trough placed there for the draft animals.

He mounted, left Marsh's camp and found the hoofprints of the fleeing cutthroat. Somehow, he wasn't all that surprised when these tracks joined those he had been following before. The rustlers' trail into the hills passed within a mile of Marsh's camp.

That might be why they had decided to chase the paleontologist away by blowing up the object of his research.

Riding into the hills, Slocum was quickly swallowed by ragged bluffs on either side of the trail. He kept looking up to the rim but saw no one on sentry duty. Mostly he studied the canyon floor and saw enough evidence that cattle had been brought this way recently to convince him that he had discovered the rustlers' main camp. The other one, where the deputy had caught him, might have been a temporary encampment or even a ruse. In his gut, Slocum knew he was on the right trail this time.

He slowed and studied the terrain ahead. The narrow passage opened to a valley. The sun had disappeared behind the high cliffs, turning the pass to twilight. In another half hour, it would be pitch dark. Slocum weighed his options. He itched to advance and find the cattle that had been stolen from the Triple Cross, but prudence dictated that he retreat and inform either the cavalry commander at Fort Bridger or the deputy marshal.

Slocum felt that too much rested on him to press ahead foolishly and take on the entire gang. He tugged on the reins and got his Appaloosa headed back down the pass so he could return to Marsh's camp and then inform the authorities.

Play it safe, he decided, though it rankled. He preferred to be in the middle of the action, not sitting on the side waiting for someone else to do his work. He had almost talked himself into going back, finding the rustlers and seeing what he could do to remedy their depredation when his horse shied.

Slocum heard a sharp crack, followed quickly by an explosion that nearly threw him from his horse. The easternmost wall of the canyon above him appeared to move in slow motion as it crept outward into space and then halted. For a single heartbeat, tons of rock defied gravity. Then gravity triumphed and the crushing mass of stone plunged downward toward him.

14

Slocum viciously spurred his horse toward the rocky canyon wall. For the span of one frenzied heartbeat, he thought he had successfully avoided most of the avalanche, then he knew he was mistaken. Badly mistaken.

A heavy rock hit him in the shoulder so hard it knocked him from horseback. Slocum hit the ground, rolled and covered his head with his arms. As more stones pelted him, he knew he couldn't stay here where he was exposed. He tried to get to hands and knees, but another rock bounced off his skull, driving him flat to the ground. Stunned, he felt tiny stones against his back like he was being hit by burning raindrops. He realized he was a goner if he didn't move fast. Scrambling for his life amid the rising cloud of choking brown dust and the tiny shards of rock flying like bullets, he got his feet under him.

Another heavy stone crashed into his back, knocking him down. This time he gasped for breath and got a mouthful of grit and dust. Eyes watering and visibility gone beyond the end of his bleeding nose, Slocum had to rely on his last impressions to figure out where safety lay.

"Wall," he grated out, refusing to die. More rock tumbled down, but some of it arced above his head, giving him hope that he was headed in the right direction. When he smashed hard against a stony barrier, he knew he had reached relative safety.

Then he worked his way along the face of the canyon wall, hunting for a crevice. Barely had he squeezed himself into the niche he'd found than the ground shook again. Slocum screamed as the rock closed around him like the jaws of a vise. Try as he might, he couldn't wiggle free. Enduring what he could not change, Slocum closed his eyes and rode out the remainder of the rock fall. Only after he realized that he heard nothing more—and that he was deaf from the horrendous clamor—did he open his eyes and look around.

The dust blew in fitful little tornados as a breeze from deeper in the canyon gusted outward. He spat and tried to get a good breath of air into his lungs. Slocum felt stabs of agony from where the rock pinned him securely. Rather than fighting to push the heavy slabs away, he began twisting back and forth until he made some small headway up the chimney. Before long, the sides widened and he tumbled outward, falling to the ground with bone-jarring force.

For several minutes Slocum lay flat on his back staring up at the distant blue Wyoming sky, wondering how he had escaped being crushed and buried. He bled from a dozen small cuts and his nose still spurted fountains of red. Using his bandanna, he stoppered his leaking nostrils and sat up. His head spun but he was still alive. Distant buzzing like bees sounded and he knew his hearing was returning.

From this point, he got to his feet and looked around. The worst of the dust had settled or blown on, letting him see the gaping cavity on the rim where the dynamite had been detonated. Slocum let out a deep breath and began brushing off the dust.

He had more than one score to settle now. That had been no accident.

When he had done the best he could to remove the cloying dust, he went in search of his horse. Slocum worried that the Appaloosa had not been fleet enough of hoof to avoid the avalanche, but he heard the horse's faint, frightened whinnying from deeper in the canyon. This worried Slocum. If he could hear the horse with his hearing impaired, that meant it was raising quite a ruckus. The sound might draw the outlaws from their hidey-hole to see if their trap had been successful. On foot, he didn't stand much chance against them. As he walked, he kept glancing up to be certain one of the rustlers wasn't there setting another charge.

"Whoa, don't go running from me," Slocum said, calming the Appaloosa as he neared it. The horse's eyes were rimmed in white, and it snorted and pawed at the rocky ground. He approached carefully, grabbed the reins and spent a few more minutes with it, until only a memory of the fear remained in the horse's brain.

Slocum started to mount but saw that the Appaloosa favored its right front leg. Pulling the hoof back caused the horse to start. Slocum went cold when he saw that the horse's leg was badly bruised. Careful probing showed no broken bones, but riding the horse in this condition was out of the question. The leg needed to be wrapped in liniment-soaked bandages and allowed a week to heal.

Slocum jerked about, listening hard when he realized that not only was his hearing returning to normal, but he heard with his usual clarity. The sound was unmistakable. Cattle lowing.

Torn between leaving his horse and investigating and slowly walking the Appaloosa back down the canyon to where he might again reach Marsh's camp safely, he made a quick, fateful decision. Slocum tied the horse's reins to a low shrub, drew his six-gun, brushed dust off it and then hurried along the rock-littered canyon floor to find the cattle. Those had to be from the Triple Cross herd.

Nobody grazed cattle in such a rocky canyon, meaning the rustlers had used this place to pen their stolen beeves.

"Get 'em all out the other end of the canyon. I don't like this place no more," called a tall, gaunt rider wearing a red-and-black checked flannel shirt and a fancy Mexican sombrero whose broad brim hid the man's face.

"Aw, Blount, we got nuthin' to worry about. That blast took care of the snoop," complained another.

Slocum's hand tightened on his six-shooter when he saw the gaunt leader reach down, lift a short-barreled shotgun and discharge both barrels into the man doing the complaining. Blount's horse reared, but he quickly regained control, knocked out the two spent shotgun shells and slammed in two more.

"Anybody else got a problem with doin' what I say?"

Four other outlaws exchanged looks, then shook their heads.

"Get the herd movin'!" shouted Blount. "I got bad feelin's 'bout this place, and when I get antsy, I get mean."

Slocum wished he had brought his Winchester. At this range he could have dropped Blount like a stone in a pond. He lifted his Colt Navy, aimed carefully and squeezed off a round. Even at fifty yards he would have hit his target if the outlaw leader's horse hadn't started crow-hopping. Slocum's bullet tore a small hole near the braid dangling at the brim of the sombrero.

This wouldn't have alerted the rustler, but the pistol report did. He thought one of his gang had decided to take him out. The sawed-off shotgun swung up and around, but he didn't immediately spot Slocum. Slocum got a second shot off and then had to dive for cover. All the other rustlers located him and shot wildly. Their rounds drilled past him harmlessly, but he did not dare take the chance that one of those frenzied shooters would accidentally hit him.

Slocum knew he had acted foolishly, but the outlaws would have disappeared along with the stolen cattle by the time he had worked his way close enough to get a good shot at Blount.

Lead tore up the vegetation around him, but Slocum didn't worry as much about being hit as he did about letting the rustlers get away. He took a deep breath, got his feet under him and then sprinted—directly at the outlaw's leader.

Blount was taken by surprise at this frontal assault. He loosed both barrels of his shotgun before Slocum was within range. Still, two streaks of lightning seared Slocum's right arm as the heavy buckshot narrowly missed him. Then he was close enough to fire. His first shot took off the outlaw's sombrero. The second hit the outlaw squarely.

"Git on outta here!" shouted Blount, doubled over and clinging to his saddle horn to keep from falling off his horse. "He got me in the gut. Shoot him!"

Slocum kept barreling ahead, safer now than he had been before. He had Blount between him and the other outlaws. If they obeyed their leader, they had to shoot past him. Slocum doubted any of them would miss Blount too much if their gunfire happened to remove him permanently, but Slocum hoped that didn't happen.

He wanted Blount alive. Slocum wanted vengeance on the man who had caused Mathiesen such trouble, who had probably murdered Chafee and who had tried to blow him up as he rode down the canyon. Holstering his Colt, Slocum put on a burst of speed that brought him alongside the wounded man's horse.

Straining, Slocum wrapped his fingers around Blount's leg and tried to pull the man down. Savage spurs raked at his face, forcing him to drop back.

"Shoot him, dammit. Shoot him!"

"You're in the way, Blount," objected another of the rustlers.

"I don't care. Shoot!"

Slocum found himself dancing about, dodging more lead than ever before. He kept grabbing for Blount, but he was losing his sheltered position. Blount cleverly wheeled his horse about so Slocum would be exposed to the other rustlers' gunfire.

When Slocum felt a sharp pain on his thigh, he knew he had lost his chance to take Blount. He whipped out his six-gun again and emptied it in the rustlers' direction. Not a single round found a target, but his quick shots scattered them and gave him another fraction of a second to stay alive.

"Damn your eyes, die!" growled Blount. The outlaw clumsily brought up his shotgun and fired. The recoil almost unseated the wounded man, but the buckshot tore at Slocum's left arm. He grabbed for his new wound. Nothing serious, but he had to get himself patched up or blood loss might become perilous.

Slocum slammed into a steer and bounced off. He saw he was at the edge of the herd, numbering at least a hundred head. Without time to reload his Colt, Slocum had to find a way to fight back. The cattle provided it.

"Hai-ya!" he shouted, waving his arms like a windmill. Slocum grabbed his hat and used it to slap one steer's rump, then moved on to a cow being trailed by her calf. He kicked at the calf and sent it running off, squealing like a pig. This produced the tumult he sought. The small herd seemed to swell and then surged, flying into a full stampede within a few yards.

The heavy dust kicked up by so many hooves choked Slocum. It also hid him from Blount and the other rustlers. The ground began to shudder under the impact of the cattle, but all Slocum wanted was to stay behind the herd.

Anyone caught in front would be trampled.

He hoped Blount and his gang were all stomped into bloody ribbons for the crimes they had committed. Slocum quickly saw that wasn't the way it had turned out. The rustlers had been forming the herd to move it out the far end of the canyon and had been to one side when he spooked the cattle. A quick count through the billowing dust showed all the rustlers still in the saddle, even if Blount rode doubled over and clutching his belly.

Slocum touched his six-shooter and considered taking time to reload. Then he knew he would miss the rustlers entirely by the time he was ready to fire. Putting his head down and running with grim determination, Slocum angled to the side of the herd to keep out of the stifling dust and then hit the rocks at the side of the trail, scrambling fast to reach the top of a big boulder at a bend in the canyon.

Seeing his chance and never hesitating, Slocum launched himself through the air to crash hard into the slowest moving rustler. The impact jarred Slocum's teeth, but it knocked the outlaw from his perch. They crashed to the ground, the man's horse kicking frantically to avoid stepping on either its rider or Slocum.

Slocum got to his feet and squared off as the rustler got to his feet, wobbling a mite. With a quick estimate of distance, Slocum stepped up and unloaded a roundhouse punch that took the rustler off his feet again. By the time the man hit the ground, he was unconscious. Slocum wasted no time stripping the varmint of his sidearm, then grabbed at the horse's dangling reins.

The rustler's horse didn't cotton much to a new rider, but Slocum clung to it like glue. Once he was in the saddle, nothing the horse did could unseat him. But the time it took him to gain control over the balky animal let the rustlers get away. The last of the cattle vanished around the bend in the canyon and, from the sounds echoing back, out onto open grassland with their pilfered herd.

"Come on," Slocum urged, putting his heels to the horse's flanks. The horse reluctantly trotted, but nothing Slocum could do brought the horse to a gallop.

He emerged from the canyon and quickly spotted the trail taken by Blount and his gang. They maneuvered the herd to the north, trying to stay in the foothills. Slocum wondered if his horse could gallop. No matter how he used the reins or his spurs, the horse refused to give him more than a brisk walk.

This saved Slocum's life. If he had ridden hell-bent for leather along the trail, he would never have seen the flash of metal high in the rocks to his left in time to duck.

A bullet sang through the air where his head had been a fraction of a second earlier.

Slocum slid off to the side of the horse, using it as a shield. Then the horse stumbled and went to its knees. A gusty sigh left its nostrils as the horse died under him. Slocum got his feet free of the stirrups before the horse collapsed entirely.

Another shot from the hidden sniper had caught the horse just above its front legs and had penetrated both lungs, killing it almost instantly. Slocum crouched behind the carcass, looking for a way to get out of the ambush. Although pinned down, he thought he could reach a tumble of rocks immediately beneath the sniper if luck smiled on him.

When he heard the sniper's rifle misfire, he sprinted hard for the spot he had picked out. It took several seconds for the rifleman to clear his chamber and lever in a new round. By then Slocum was immediately under his position, where the drygulcher couldn't get a good shot at him. Slocum clutched his captured pistol and looked up, wondering how long this stalemate would last.

He saw a faint game trail leading around the rocks and up to where the sniper lay, but if he took it he would walk straight into the man's sights. Slocum went the other way, struggling through a large clump of prickly pear and then Spanish bayonet before getting to the spot where he could get the drop on the gunman.

Slocum braced himself, then whirled around and leveled his six-shooter at . . . empty space.

The sound of a six-shooter cocking from behind told Slocum he had misjudged his opponent and was now going to pay for this mistake with his life.

15

Slocum cursed his carelessness. He had committed a greenhorn's mistake of jumping at a sound rather than being certain what danger was all around him.

"I ought to drill you where you stand," came a curiously familiar voice. The precise clipped tones convinced Slocum he could take a chance. A big one, but he had no choice. He thrust his hands high in the air, still clutching the six-shooter, and then turned to face his assailant.

"You are the cause of too much trouble for me not to kill you," sputtered Edward Cope. The man's six-gun wobbled as a fit of rage seized him. His face turned red with anger, and he looked as if he might pop his cork at any instant.

Slocum took in everything with a flash of intuition. Cope hadn't tried to shoot him from above. That sniper had used a rifle.

"Above us!" Slocum looked up, feinted with his body and then moved fast to get out of Cope's line of fire.

Cope reacted to the unexpected warning as Slocum had hoped. The man whirled about, his attention drawn in the direction Slocum pointed. Slocum had already cast a quick glance above and decided the sniper had pulled out, his dirty work done. The hidden rifleman had intended for Cope and Slocum to shoot each other. If one or the other survived, he probably didn't care. Confusion would have been sown, and any survivor would be tracked down by the deputy federal marshal.

Slocum lowered his six-shooter and aimed it squarely at the paleontologist.

"Don't make me shoot," Slocum said in a steely voice. He cocked his gun when Cope tried to bring his own weapon to bear again. "I'm a good shot. At this range, I won't miss."

Slocum saw Cope's mind working on unaccustomed problems of speed, accuracy and what to expect from a determined man holding a six-shooter on him with an unwavering aim.

"You ought to be strung up!" Cope cried, his voice going shrill in his anger. "I should have shot you when I had the chance. Well, go on! Kill me. It's what you do, isn't it, Slocum?"

"I've shot a man or two in my day," Slocum allowed. "Drop your hogleg so we can talk."

Cope's anger turned into confusion.

"The gun. Drop it," Slocum explained when he saw that the Easterner didn't understand him. Cope reluctantly obeyed.

"That's better," Slocum went on. "I was chasing rustlers when they almost blew me to hell and gone. The canyon wall came crashing down on me and hurt my horse. I needed another to go after the gang. I was fetching one when you interrupted me."

"Gangs, rustlers, horses—you're lying!" Cope began pacing to and fro like a caged animal. "What's any of that mean? You're a criminal. You blew up my precious specimen. You stole away my finest fossil evidence."

"How'd I do a thing like that?"

"Dynamite, that's how. You blew up the dinosaur skeleton so thoroughly not even my genius can piece it back together. Weeks of work ruined in a flash." He threw his hands up, as if retracing the path taken by the explosion. Cope stopped pacing as his anger returned.

Slocum's mind worked like lightning on what the scientist said. Answers came and he doubted Cope wanted to hear them.

"They're playing us off against one another. The rustlers are responsible for stealing dynamite from the Triple Cross Ranch; then they used some on Marsh's specimens. I thought they had done it because his dig was too near the path leading into this canyon, but I don't think that was it. Not entirely. They wanted to get him riled."

"But it was my fossil skeleton that was destroyed so utterly! You're talking nonsense. Marsh is responsible. You and Marsh!"

"Your skeleton and his skeleton were destroyed," Slocum said. "You blame him, Marsh blames you. And they are stealing Triple Cross cattle. The rustlers killed the foreman, and they just tried to kill me with a couple more sticks of dynamite. They're dangerous, Cope. They aren't content with just stealing. They're starting a range war for the sheer pleasure of watching us shoot each other."

"What difference does any of that make? Someone destroyed my dinosaur skeleton before I had a chance to evaluate it properly and determine the precise classification. Why, it might be a tyrannosaurus or some smaller predator, an allosaurus, mayhap. Or—"

"Shut up," Slocum said, not caring to hear a learned lecture about dry bones painstakingly clawed from the Wyoming rock. He had to punctuate his order with motion from his six-shooter. Only then did Cope subside and glower at him.

"I want you to listen carefully to what I'm going to say," Slocum went on.

"If I don't?"

"I'll plug you where you stand. That'll mean the rustlers have won, but I won't give a good tenpenny damn about it since you'll be quiet." Slocum saw that this confounded Cope. The man clamped his mouth shut and glared. For the moment, this was good enough for Slocum. "This gang is playing with us all like a cat toying with a trapped mouse. They steal cattle for profit, but they have a mean streak a mile wide and enjoy causing trouble between you and Marsh. The more you shoot at him, the more the rustlers like the spectacle."

From everything Slocum had seen, it hadn't taken much to stir up old enmities. The two men had been academic rivals back East. Adding a bit of hot lead and the dynamite had only pushed the fight to a new, more deadly level. He imagined the rustler named Blount sitting back and giving a good belly laugh as the two expeditions went after one another, stealing and shooting and sabotaging each other's hard work. The worst part was that both Marsh and Cope were blind to the subterfuge, since they already hated each other so completely.

Mix in the deputy marshal from Kemmerer and maybe even the cavalry detachment at Fort Bridger, and the rustlers had everyone in the territory stirred up and doing everything imaginable—except capturing outlaws.

Slocum pictured the shot that had sent a slug into Blount's belly and felt a bit of vindication. The outlaw leader might not have been the one who personally killed Chafee, but he had organized the ambush. That murder had the same sort of sneakiness about it as the idea of setting one Easterner against the other.

"What are you going to do? Kill me where I stand? You might as well, since you're Marsh's henchman. Go on. Earn your blood money," Cope said, firing up his invective against Marsh again. He thrust out his chest in a dramatic pose, daring Slocum to shoot.

"Shut up," Slocum said. "I'm not going to kill you. In

fact, I'm sending you back to your camp." He paused and frowned. "What were you doing here, anyway? You almost rode into the middle of the rustlers' camp."

"I was hunting for a new fossil find to rival the one you so imprudently revealed to Marsh. That particular fossil bed might prove to be the greatest find of the century, and *he* will be the one claiming it, writing of it, garnering the public accolades and displaying the fruits of the past in his execrable museum."

Slocum felt bile rising in his mouth. This meant Marsh had started digging up the Arapaho burial ground again, in spite of the warning to avoid the area. Slocum felt as if he were a fireman with a small bucket of water, turning this way and that to throw what little he could on raging fires all around him. One blaze died down, only to have another surge out of control.

The thought flashed through his mind that letting Marsh and Cope kill each other might be the only way to bring peace back to the territory. He discarded this quickly as the illusion of tranquillity faded. There would never be peace in the land. If Marsh and Cope weren't shooting at each other, the Arapahos would be stealing Mathiesen's cattle or raiding wagon trains. And the rustlers had found a gold mine to exploit in Triple Cross cattle with Mathiesen ill and most of his cowboys inexperienced.

Besides, if Cope and Marsh succeeded in killing each other, where would that leave Ella Weedin? Slocum found himself thinking of her and her clever drawings.

"I'll take your horse," Slocum said. "Where is it?" He saw the direction Cope involuntarily looked and knew that the paleontologist had left his horse at the far side of the canyon, coming over on foot to see what the shooting was all about.

"That's horse theft. I may not know the ways of this land, but I know enough to realize they hang men for that, Slocum. I ought to see you strung up!"

"Shut up," Slocum said mechanically. It was the only command Edward Cope obeyed, although never long enough for Slocum to appreciate the silence. "You'll take my Appaloosa back to your camp and tend him. When I've finished tracking down the rustlers, we can trade horses again."

"What's wrong with your horse?" Cope asked.

"Bruised leg. You can't ride him, but he can hobble along just fine as long as you don't rush him." Slocum doubted the rustlers had remained in the area for long, not with their leader gut-shot and the lone sniper content that he had created all the strife he could with his few well-placed rounds. It was as if the rustlers tossed a rattler into the center of a camp and then ran off without waiting to see how many poor souls got bit. The only bright spot Slocum could see was that Blount getting shot might have put a damper on their enthusiasm for creating mischief.

"If I let you keep your six-gun, will you promise not to go hunting Marsh?"

"No!"

It was as Slocum had feared. Cope had a one-track mind, and all he knew was besting his academic rival, either by word or by bullet.

"If you touch the pistol, I'll put a bullet through your hand," Slocum warned as Cope bent to reach for the gun. "You won't need that on the way back to your camp."

"But I might see a snake," Cope protested. His lip curled as he added, "One named Othniel Marsh!"

"Get moving. I don't want to give the rustlers any more of a head start than they have already." Slocum kept his six-gun pointed at Cope as the man bustled off on the direction Slocum had indicated, where the Appaloosa stood restlessly, painfully waiting. Letting Cope deal with the injured animal rankled, but Slocum felt the pressure on him like the ton of rocks that had barely missed killing him. He wanted to find the outlaw leader.

He had to.

Slocum owed Chafee.

Cope went off, grumbling and looking back over his shoulder as he went to retrieve the Appaloosa. Slocum slid the six-gun into his broad belt and then took time to reload his Colt. He scooped up the gun Cope had dropped and added this to his arsenal. Only then did he make his way through the rocks to where Cope had left his horse. Slocum swung into the saddle, wincing as he did so. Only now did the myriad cuts and scratches he had accumulated begin to bother him. Most had scabbed over and weren't anywhere near as serious as he had worried earlier. Forcing the minor pains from his mind, he turned the horse's face toward the large rock where the sniper had lain in wait.

It took him only a few minutes to pick up the trail and begin following it. Slocum reckoned that the outlaw knew where the gang's rendezvous was and would head there straightaway to boast of his sharpshooting. He wasn't disappointed when he found a great number of hoofprints from cattle. Stolen cattle.

Slocum rode faster now, like a bloodhound on a scent. He kept his attention focused ahead and to the rims of the canyon on either side, to keep from blundering into another ambush, but the steep walls gradually backed off and widened, until a broad, grassy mountain meadow stretched in front of him.

"Damn fine grazing here," he said to himself. The horse he rode wanted to graze, but Slocum kept it moving. Following the trail was easy for him, although he worried he would overtake the remaining rustlers and find himself in an unexpected gunfight. He would be up against at least four men willing to kill anything that moved. The sniper who had taken the potshot at Slocum would be especially eager to finish the job begun back deep in the canyon.

Slocum slowed and then halted. Cope's horse took the

opportunity to try to buck him off, but Slocum was too good a rider to let the horse have its way. He studied the ground as he tugged on the reins, eyes lifting to the center of the valley where the stolen cattle had been herded.

A single set of hoofprints cut away, going toward a stand of scrub oak. What caught Slocum's attention was the occasional lump of bloody mud.

"Blount," he said, a coldness settling on him. "You're going to find out the meaning of justice."

He put his heels to the horse and trotted after Blount, warier than ever as he neared the trees. This was a perfect spot for an ambush, but when he saw Blount's horse peacefully grazing he knew he wasn't riding into a trap.

Slocum slid from the saddle and drew the two six-shooters shoved into his belt.

"Blount!" he bellowed. "Come on out. We got a fight to finish."

Slocum advanced to the nearest broad-leafed tree and sneaked a quick peek around. Blount sat on a stump not twenty feet away, clutching his pistol and trying not to topple over. He looked up and saw Slocum. Gripping the six-gun in both hands, he got off a shot, but the recoil knocked him off his perch.

Slocum stepped out and blazed away. Splinters flew from the stump, and one round caught Blount in the arm. His six-shooter went sailing from his weakened grip, leaving him helpless on the ground.

"Your partners left you, Blount," Slocum taunted. "They left you to die."

"I give up. I surrender. Don't shoot," the outlaw called as he struggled to sit up.

Slocum saw the outlaw lift his hands the best he could. The front of the rustler's shirt was soaked with blood from Slocum's first shot in the gut. His right sleeve dripped with fresh blood from the second wound.

"Don't shoot me," Blount grated out, his teeth

clenched. "You shot me good. Don't kill me."

"This is for Chafee, you son of a bitch," Slocum said.

Slocum lifted the six-gun in his right hand, aimed between the outlaw's eyes and pulled the trigger.

16

The hammer of Slocum's captured six-shooter fell with a dull *clack!* on a spent chamber. He threw the pistol away and lifted the six-gun in his left hand, aimed and saw Blount along the barrel, the front knife-sight splitting the rustler's forehead in a perfectly aimed shot. For a moment, Slocum paused, and then he lowered the weapon, cursing himself for his change of heart.

"I'm taking you to the deputy marshal. If there's any justice in Wyoming Territory, he'll see to it that they put a noose around your neck and hang you so high it'll take a month of Sundays for you to fall when they cut you down."

Blount clutched his abdomen, looking up at Slocum with feverish eyes. His blanched face told what he thought of almost dying at Slocum's hand.

"Keep pressing into that belly wound," Slocum said. "You might not bleed to death by the time we get to Kemmerer."

"Go on, kill me. You tried. You got the nerve for it. I knowed it when I saw your eyes. Don't let me live to stand trial."

If anything, this hardened Slocum's resolve to turn

145

Blount over to Deputy Gaines. Blount didn't deserve an easy death.

"Get your horse. If you can't ride, I'll tie you across the saddle like a sack of flour."

"I . . . I can ride." Blount forced himself to his feet and staggered. Slocum watched carefully to be certain the rustler wasn't trying to pull a fast one. He knew he should search him for a hideout gun, a derringer or a small knife, but so much blood flowed from both stomach and arm that Slocum didn't want to bother.

Blount got his horse and struggled into the saddle. He sagged forward and, for a moment, Slocum thought the outlaw had died. Then the rustler let out a tiny moan of pain and got his horse moving slowly. Slocum grabbed at the reins and led the horse to where he had left Cope's.

As they rode back through the canyon and the avalanche-blocked section of the trail, Slocum kept a sharp eye out for the rest of the gang. They had driven the stolen cattle through into the grassy valley and were nowhere to be seen, but Slocum found questions building up he had to ask.

"Why'd you split away from the rest of your gang back there?" he asked.

Blount grunted, stirred and shook himself from his red haze of pain.

"Couldn't keep up. Wanted to die in the trees. Always liked oak trees, even scrub oak. Don't wanna die in jail. Don't make me."

"You killed Chafee," Slocum said coldly. "You're going to pay for that. And for stealing Triple Cross cattle. Maybe there are a dozen other crimes waiting to be pinned on you, too, but it's Chafee's death that's going to stretch your good-for-nothing neck. And if the rest of your gang would let you die alone, they sure as hell aren't going to rescue you."

"Don't know any Chafee," the rustler said. He turned

his head and spat blood. "The rest of my boys, they knowed what we was about. Any of us get hurt real bad, they get left. That goes for me, too. A wounded man'll slow everyone down and we'd all get caught."

"Chafee was the Triple Cross foreman," Slocum went on relentlessly. He didn't care about whatever code drove the outlaws. All that mattered was finding a way for Chafee to rest easy in his grave. "You laid an ambush for him. He was a good man and you murdered him."

Slocum saw that his words failed to sting Blount. The outlaw drifted away into a world racked with pain.

They came out of the mouth of the canyon. To his right lay Marsh's camp, but Slocum avoided it and the explanations of how he had come to capture the gang leader. It was a considerable ride northeast to Kemmerer, but Slocum started without giving Blount a chance to rest. Considering the man's weakened condition, if he tried to rest too much, he might just up and die. Slocum wanted him locked up in Gaines's jail before that happened.

Less than twenty minutes after emerging from the canyon mouth, Slocum felt the hairs on the back of his neck begin to twitch and stand. Such feelings had kept him alive during the war and after. He always paid them heed. Without being too obvious, he reached over and laid his hand on his Colt Navy. Barely had he touched the cool ebony handle when a pair of bullets tore through the air, coming at him from different directions.

One gunman lay to his right, behind a towering clump of prickly pear cactus, and the other hid to his oblique left, amid waist-high grass. At first Slocum thought he had ridden smack into another ambush, but the rounds that followed weren't as much directed at him as they were sent wildly through the air.

"Get down," Slocum ordered Blount. The rustler didn't stir as he slumped forward over his saddlebow. Slocum slid from his horse and went to grab Blount so he could drag him to safety, but the rustler had been playing possum. He kicked out powerfully and sent Slocum staggering backward. Catching a heel, Slocum sat down heavily and dropped his Colt. This was all the break Blount needed to bend low, put his spurs to his horse and rocket away.

Slocum grabbed for his six-shooter, but new shots tore through the air just overhead. He lay flat, wiggled like a snake and retrieved his gun. By the time he dared to look up, Blount was long gone.

But the men shooting at each other weren't. They filled the Wyoming grasslands with gunfire that rolled like deadly thunder into the distance. What puzzled Slocum was their inept marksmanship. A lot of lead flew, but none of it was well aimed.

"Hold your fire!" Slocum barked. "I'm standing up. Don't shoot!"

He slowly got to his feet and faced the six-foot-high mound of cactus.

"Come on out," Slocum shouted, wondering who would emerge. It didn't surprise him when Othniel Marsh came out, a rifle clutched in his shaking hands. Slocum turned to the spot in the grass where he had spotted the other gunman. "You, too, Cope. This fight's over."

"He blew up my specimen!" Edward Cope came out, another six-shooter held in his wavering grip.

The two scientists were such bad gunmen Slocum wondered how they had avoided shooting themselves by accident.

"You let the leader of the rustlers escape," Slocum said, his words hot with emotion. "I was taking him to the deputy marshal's lockup in Kemmerer and you blazed away at me."

"I protest, Mr. Slocum!" cried Marsh. "I had no idea you were within a dozen miles. My shots were directed at *him*. He fired upon me and I was only defending myself."

"Defending yourself? You shot at *me* first, you lying—"

Slocum pointed his Colt at the sky and fired a single round to get their attention. It worked. Barely.

"Quiet down, both of you. You're both a menace to anyone riding along peaceably. I don't care what you do to each other, but you can't keep trading lead without hitting someone you don't intend to kill."

"I intend to kill him," Cope said.

"I'll get you!" warned Marsh.

Slocum fired another shot into the air.

"The two of you, put your weapons down. I swear, I'll kill you where you stand if you don't do it. Now!"

The men jumped as if he had stuck them with a pin.

"Good," Slocum said, seeing that both had obeyed him. "This is none of my business, but I'm going to stop your feud right now."

"You can't! You favor that charlatan. Marsh steals and robs and you gave him the best site in all of Wyoming!"

"That's an Indian burial ground and is off limits to both of you." Slocum looked from one to the other. "Dig there and you'll regret it. The Arapahos will lift the scalps of every white man south of the Yellowstone River. I warned you away once, Marsh, and now I'm doing it again—for the last time. If the Indians don't kill you for digging in their cemetery, I will."

"You can't expect us to give up our hunt," protested Marsh. Cope quickly echoed his rival's sentiment. Slocum had found something they agreed on.

"I know where you can find better fossils than your current locations—both of your locations, including the Arapaho burial grounds. If I show you, will you dig in peace and not shoot at each other?"

Cope and Marsh glared at each other, then sullenly nodded. Slocum reckoned the feud was a goodly part of what kept both men going. They might prattle on about academic study and piecing together the bones of long dead, completely unlikely animals, but their mutual animosity gave them passion and put meaning into their lives.

"I won't give one a better site than the other," Slocum said, not knowing what that meant. To him, bones were bones and ought to be left in the ground.

"Where?" demanded Cope.

"You know the spot in the canyon where I was almost buried alive?" Slocum saw the scientist nod. "There were bones in the strata revealed by the explosion."

"I never noticed since I came in from another direction," Cope said, rubbing his hands together. He turned to Marsh. "You don't get to study what I unearth, you—"

Before he could find the proper insult to cut deeply into another fragile psyche, Slocum interrupted. "And you, Professor, beyond the rockfall is the rustlers' old camp. They left in a hurry and probably paid no attention to the rocks around them. Bones. Tons of them."

"In the canyon walls or on the floor?" asked Marsh, intrigued in spite of himself.

"On the floor," Slocum said, wondering why this made a difference. But it obviously did because Marsh began gloating.

"My site is older!"

Slocum separated the pair, sending them to find their horses. He was happy to see that Cope had not tried to ride the Appaloosa left in his care. A few minutes' questioning got the information from Cope that he had come across his foreman and sent the hobbling horse back with him, while taking Leigh's horse to strike out in search of new paleontological sites.

Slocum rode between the men, keeping them from directly addressing each other.

"How'd you both come to be out alone?" he finally

asked, finding he boiled over with questions, as he had with Blount.

"I don't trust any of the others in my camp," Cope said with startling candor. "He has bribed and threatened the men working for me to the point I am unable to trust them. I wanted to find a good field to excavate without the information leaking to *him*." Edward Cope looked so smug that Slocum wanted to reach over and lay his pistol barrel alongside the man's head.

Slocum turned to Marsh and read much the same reason for the solitary excursion. Professor Marsh didn't trust any of his crew, either. But that's not what he said.

Nose tilted upward slightly to show his disdain, Marsh said, "My expertise is such that only I can determine the proper spot to dig."

Slocum started to point out that he had no idea what they wanted in the bones and yet had found sites that excited both men. More than this, most of the professor's workers were students capable of locating the spots as easily as Marsh. He simply did not want to share the glory of discovery with anyone.

"This trail," Othniel Marsh said, frowning. "This is where the rustlers drove the stolen cattle, isn't it?" He craned about in the saddle, shielded his eyes against the sun and squinted along the backtrail toward his own camp, a few miles distant.

"The cattle went all the way down the canyon into a valley beyond," Slocum said, champing at the bit to be riding across that grassy meadow on Blount's trail. The leader of the rustlers had to find help for his wounds soon or he would die. As badly wounded as he was, Blount would only create a stir and generate questions he would never want asked if he rode to Fort Bridger or even Kemmerer.

As much as bringing Blount to justice, Slocum wanted to recover some of the cattle the outlaws had been so aggressively stealing from the Triple Cross. Mr. Mathiesen could ill afford the losses, and returning the beeves to his pastures would go a ways toward turning a profit for the year.

"Mr. Slocum, as I live and breathe, you were right!" exclaimed Cope. He shot forward, ignoring Marsh's protests. Slocum held the other scientist back as Cope hurriedly dismounted and began scrambling up the rubble that had been dynamited from the canyon rim. Cope ran his fingers over raw rock, outlining bones jutting from the side of the canyon.

"This might be a major find," Marsh said angrily. He glared at Slocum. "I thought you were inclined to support my search, and yet you gave him a find of this magnitude. I do not understand you."

"Forget this," Slocum said. "Let Cope have his fun. I'll show you a real spot to dig up these dinosaur burial grounds." He rode past the cooing Edward Cope, with Marsh following sullenly.

Slocum rode directly to the spot where the outlaw camp had been. Here and there abandoned fire pits still smoldered.

"Well? Where . . ." Marsh's voice trailed off when he saw what Slocum had earlier. He jumped to the ground and then dropped to his knees, brushing furiously to get pine needles, leaves and other detritus away from a rocky shelf.

"Yes, yes, this *is* nice. Why, it might provide an entire skeleton." Marsh looked up and smiled broadly. "I must get Miss Weedin here immediately to sketch the area. I need a complete record of the bone distribution. I'll show him. I'll really show him!"

Slocum didn't have to ask whom the scientist meant. For Marsh the only possible rival in the world was Edward Cope. And for Cope, no greater villain existed than Othniel Marsh.

Slocum left the two at their preliminary explorations and once more rode the trail to the valley at the far end of the canyon. He had cattle to recover and a gang of rustlers to bring to justice.

Especially their leader.

17

Slocum spent two days ranging through the grassy valley hunting for the rustlers, to no avail. He found traces of a temporary camp and more than a few tracks from the herd of stolen cattle moved along at a brisk pace, but he lost all signs of both outlaws and cattle at the far end of the valley when they vanished into twisting mazes of canyons.

As chagrined as Slocum was over not even sighting the rustlers, he felt good about his exploration of the valley. This was a fine place for Triple Cross cattle to fatten up. Ample water pooled for a hundred times the number of cattle Mathiesen owned, and the protection of the mountains surrounding the valley would make this a good place to winter the herd.

But Slocum had failed to stop the rustlers. Worse, he had no idea if Blount was dead or alive. He hoped the man had died a painful death after he had escaped, but in his gut Slocum knew that wasn't so. Blount was the kind of bad penny who would return again and again.

Carefully mapping his way back to the Triple Cross, Slocum came across Tatum and three cowboys several miles from the ranch house.

"Hey, Mr. Slocum!" called Tatum, looking pleased as punch about something. "We figgered you was long gone. Glad to see you're back. Mr. Mathiesen's been askin' after you, and I didn't know what all to say."

"I found a good place to graze the cattle, summer and winter," Slocum said. "Might be a tad hard getting the beeves up there since the canyons are narrow, but once there, they'll put on weight in jig time."

"If there're any beeves left," Tatum said, turning more somber. "Them rustlers've been workin' hard to thin our herd, Mr. Slocum."

Slocum stewed over this. He had settled the feud, at least to the point where they weren't shooting at each other, between Cope and Marsh, but the problem posed by the rustlers festered like an open saddle sore.

"Any trouble with the Arapahos?" he asked.

"Been wavin' to that one what's their war chief when we pass, and he seems like a friendly enough fellow," Tatum said. "Burning Knife's the name."

"That's good. The fewer bullets flying, the more likely we can get down to the business of raising cattle."

"I ain't seen hide nor hair of that deputy marshal from up north," Tatum said. "He was supposed to be huntin' them rustlers, but he's vanished from the face of the earth."

"You're doing a good job," Slocum congratulated the youngster. "From the look of it, as good as I could do."

"Aw, you're jist sayin' that," Tatum said, but he was obviously pleased at the compliment. "What I don't know, I jist sorta make up as I go. Been workin', too."

"That's the secret," Slocum said. "Nobody knows all the answers, so we have to figure them out as we ride along." Slocum shifted in the saddle, aware that Tatum was staring at the broken-down old horse and wondering what had become of the Appaloosa. Slocum was in need of some patching up from all his scratches, and a long bath wouldn't be amiss, either.

" 'Cept for them rustlers, no problems to solve," Tatum declared. "Mr. Mathiesen lets us be, him bein' so sick and all, and the missus fixes her mighty fine victuals."

"Keep on doing what you're doing," Slocum said. "I have to return this horse and track down the rustlers. If Deputy Gaines isn't doing anything about them, somebody has to."

"You said you ain't havin' much luck, though," Tatum said. "We surely can use you back tellin' us what to do. We lost three more hands to the Montana goldfields."

"I know where I might find a few riders, but it'll be a spell before they could take a job," Slocum said, thinking of the workers on both fossil hunting expeditions. When Cope and Marsh left to return east, a goodly number of the men in their employ would need jobs. A few had the look of cowboys. The rest were students and would return to school with Marsh.

"We can keep goin' with what we have, considerin' how the herd's gettin' smaller," Tatum said. "No reflection on you, Mr. Slocum, but maybe we oughta get them soldiers onto the rustlers' trail."

"Have Mr. Mathiesen send a letter to the post commander," Slocum said, "but if they haven't been hunting for the rustlers, there's no reason for the bluecoats to go now. Might be a benefit to convince them Burning Knife is peaceable and there's no need to watch for an Arapaho uprising."

"Anything I kin do for you, Mr. Slocum?" Tatum asked.

"Keep doing your job." Slocum laughed without humor, then smiled, leaned over and slapped Tatum on the back. "Keep doing my job."

Satisfied that the Triple Cross was in good hands, Slocum wheeled his horse around and headed for the canyon mouth, where Edward Cope worked to uncover entire skeletons.

He approached the scientist slowly, seeing Cope and a half dozen others working diligently with picks and shovels to move not only the rock that had fallen but also rock from the face of the canyon wall. Slocum marveled at how Cope looked so fresh and clean amid the rising clouds of dust as his crew worked. Cope wore a new cravat, a bright red silk one wrapped around a starched collar so stiff it held his head immobile and made him look as if he perpetually looked down his nose at the world.

From all Slocum had seen, Cope probably did look askance at the world that had nothing to do with bones. Now that he had discovered a new bone field, his world was perfect.

Cope's foreman, Leigh, came over and wiped sweat off his face. He leaned on his shovel and looked up at Slocum.

"That's one of our horses," he said without greeting.

"Does Cope pay you to goldbrick?" Slocum asked in an equally nasty tone.

"Mr. Slocum!" cried Cope, hurrying over. He stroked his beard constantly and beamed. "This is a find of the first water. Splendid, perfectly splendid."

"And you're finding dinosaurs that Marsh never will," Slocum said sarcastically. Leigh glared at him, but Cope missed the implied message.

"I'll beat him to publication again, as I have so many times before. I will be lionized in academic circles while he is still pondering over some esoteric point. Yes, yes, this is a major find. Thank you for pointing it out to me, Mr. Slocum."

"I brought back your horse. How's my Appaloosa?"

"The gimpy horse?" asked Leigh.

The foreman swallowed hard when he saw how Slocum

shifted in the saddle so his hand moved closer to the handle of his Colt Navy.

"Uh, the nag's doing fine," Leigh hastily said.

"A fine horse, and I ordered special care for it, Mr. Slocum," said Cope. "As a tribute to you for helping me in finding this marvel of the Cretaceous Epoch."

Slocum dismounted and handed the reins to Leigh. The foreman took them reluctantly and went to fetch Slocum's horse and gear.

"How long do you intend to dig?" Slocum asked, seeing all of Cope's men hard at work.

"It's hard to say, because I am having great difficulty finding wagons large enough to transport my dinosaur skeletons. The bones must be carefully packed for transport back East, of course, but no one in Fort Bridger has a spare wagon. I find this very strange, but it permits me extra time to unearth still more bones."

Leigh returned with the Appaloosa. Slocum took a few minutes to run his fingers over the injured leg, probing gently. The horse showed no sign of tenderness. The sharp scent of liniment gave further evidence that Leigh had followed his boss's instructions. Slocum patted the horse on the neck and turned back to the paleontologist, who still prattled on about how successful this trip was and how he would move the skeletons when he found the proper wagons.

"I'll see if I can find a wagon or two for you to move out these bones," Slocum said. The sooner Cope sent his treasure trove of bleached ribs back East, the sooner he would leave Wyoming. Somehow, Slocum liked the idea of there being one fewer bone-obsessed man digging up the ground and chiseling away at the faces of cliffs.

"Much obliged, yes, thank you," Cope said, not having heard what Slocum said. Leigh started to speak, but Slocum had already mounted and rode away. Slocum had no reason to listen to anything either of the men said.

He rode deeper into the canyon, down the winding ways, and eventually came out into the flatter widening where the rustlers had pitched their camp.

Slocum let out a low whistle of surprise. Before, there had been a few trees scattered about the grassy area. All trace of where the outlaws had penned the stolen cattle was gone—as were the trees. Othniel Marsh had cleared the area of any distraction from digging his pits. Most of the excavations were waist-deep now, his men straining mightily in the hot sun. His foreman, Sanborn, worked to lay out grid patterns made from stakes and string on an area newly scraped clean.

A tent pitched to the far side of the work area drew Slocum. No one called to him or even noticed him, because they were so intent on their chores. Slocum dismounted and pulled back the tent flap. At a small table inside struggled a frantic looking Othniel Marsh. He jerked about, looking up with wide eyes when he felt the breeze from outside blowing into the tent.

"Mr. Slocum! I hadn't expected to see you again. Come in."

Slocum settled on the man's cot before speaking. He took in everything about the tent and remembered how it had looked in General Jim Longstreet's tent before a minor skirmish when he had been an acting courier during the war. The atmosphere was as tense and the tent as disordered.

"You look like you're up against it. Anything wrong?"

"Wrong?" The expression on Marsh's face went through confusion and finally settled on a foolish looking smile. "How can anything be wrong? This is the find of the century! Not even Professor Mudge has located such an array of fine specimens. You are to be commended for giving them to me rather than that charlatan, Cope."

"You look upset," Slocum said.

"Upset? No, I am rushed! There is so much happening,

so much that needs to be done. I have only a few more weeks before I must return to Yale. The fall semester will commence then, and I need to put all these fine skeletons together for a proper exhibition. I will make the Peabody Museum preeminent in the world, thanks to you."

"So you're leaving soon?" asked Slocum. "How are you getting the bones out of here?" He saw the sly look and knew then why Cope was having such a difficult time finding transportation for his own dinosaur skeletons.

"I have a small, uh, wagon train, I believe the term is, coming in through that valley you found. I shall pack the dinosaurs carefully and ship them to Kemmerer. From there, it is only a matter of finding the proper railhead to complete the journey east."

"You're not going back to Fort Bridger?"

"No," Marsh said, looking even shiftier.

"That'd mean you'd have to move your wagons past Cope's dig," Slocum said, supplying the reason. "And you've cornered the market on wagons in southwestern Wyoming."

"That's putting it a bit strongly, my good man," Marsh said, but the feral grin he flashed Slocum told the story. In spite of both researchers having finds worthy of their talents, the old animosity still burned brightly.

"It's cooler working here than out on the grasslands," Slocum said, "but the snow comes sooner." He knew it would be several months before the weather became a problem, but he wanted to goad Marsh on his way.

"We shall be long gone before the snows bury this site," Marsh assured him.

"Will you be back next year?"

The professor laughed. "You fear I will disrupt your cattle raising again? Fear not, sir. I have other spots I wish to explore. In the Dakota Badlands and in . . . other places." From the way he avoided naming it, Slocum reckoned Marsh wanted to send Cope north while he explored in some other direction.

"Colorado's got mighty fine mountains, too," Slocum said. From the stricken look on Marsh's face, he knew he had named the next search area. Slocum vowed to go neither north nor south but to continue to the coast so he could avoid the two paleontologists and their mindless enmity.

The Arapahos were quieting down. Cope and Marsh would be leaving soon. That left Slocum with the problem of Blount and his gang of rustlers. Then all that would be left was overseeing the workings of the Triple Cross Ranch.

All, he thought, knowing this was a full-time, demanding job. The scientists and their crews, the Indians and even the rustlers were only distractions from a more difficult chore.

Then something occurred to him that he had only danced around before.

"What's going to become of Miss Weedin?" he asked.

Marsh had already turned back to making crabbed notations on his map of the canyon floor where his crew excavated so painstakingly. The scientist muttered something, then looked up at Slocum.

"Ella's off in the valley, waiting to direct the wagons in this direction when they arrive. She is also working on a series of sepia sketches of the smaller maxillary bones taken from . . ."

Slocum was already out the tent. He cared nothing about learned discussions of the chalky bones pulled from the ground, but seeing Ella again would do his spirits a world of good.

He had intended to retrieve his horse, then see when the scientists were moving on, then go into the very valley where Ella had been sent. He hoped that the rustlers were far away and posed no threat to the woman. The more he worried as he rode, the less certain he was that she was safe. Blount had used both canyon and valley to hide his stolen beeves. He might decide this territory was all his and be willing to shoot anyone intruding again.

Slocum worried even more that Blount wasn't as likely to shoot Ella as he was to do even worse if he captured her.

Sudden sunlight blinded Slocum for a moment as he left the steep-walled canyon and went once more into the broad, grassy valley. He sucked in a settling breath and set to tracking the artist. Riding a fan-shaped route, he soon found recent hoofprints that led from the canyon. He followed easily, then noticed how the tracks led to the same stand of trees where he had captured Blount. Slocum began to wonder if he had picked up the wrong set of tracks and again trailed the leader of the rustlers.

That would be fine with him, since it would eliminate a great deal of danger for Ella, should she be somewhere else in the valley.

Then he entered the clearing where he had drawn a bead on Blount, only to find the six-gun he had used was empty.

A horse nibbled contentedly at the far side of the grassy expanse. Slocum rode past the stump where Blount had tried to summon enough strength to shoot him, saw the bloodstains on the wood and ground, then rode so he could let his Appaloosa graze beside what was unmistakably Ella's horse.

Slocum cocked his head to one side when he heard faint words drifting through the trees. He followed the sound until he came to one of the pools that would serve so well for watering the Triple Cross herd.

Ella Weedin sang in a clear, sweet voice as she splashed about in the pool unaware anyone was within a dozen miles.

Slocum knew he shouldn't spy on her, but he couldn't

help himself. As she rolled over on her back in the water, her firm, fine breasts poked up to present two pink-capped snowy mounds that seemed to float on their own. Her long legs kicked gracefully, coming out of the water just enough to keep her moving as she drifted in the pool, eyes closed and oblivious to the world.

Her arms swished back and forth to maintain her position in the center of the pond, and occasional scissoring movements of her legs revealed the wetted auburn patch between her thighs. Everything about the beautiful woman appealed to Slocum. He had not thought their paths would cross again when they'd parted the last time—or had he? Slocum was certain that the wanton artist had wanted them to meet again. He could not get her mischievous smile out of his mind.

Slocum shed his coat, vest and shirt, then began shucking off the rest of his clothes behind the curtain of brush along the edge of the pond. Buck naked, he moved to the edge of the water and waited to see if Ella was aware of his presence. She gave no indication she knew he was there. Sucking in a deep breath, Slocum cut the water smoothly, dove deep and slipped along the mud-slick bottom of the pool, swimming strongly to reach the middle of the water.

He twisted about and looked up to see Ella's delightful figure framed by rippling water and the pure blue Wyoming sky. She moved her arms and legs slightly to keep afloat, but the sight of her firm, rounded buttocks and the occasional glimpse of her breasts as she bobbed about robbed Slocum of his intention to approach slowly.

More than needing air, he needed the woman.

Slocum surged upward, whirling about in the water to come up under her. His chest pressed firmly against her back and his legs rose between hers as the woman's creamy thighs parted.

Ella reacted in a way totally unexpected. She reached

down between her legs and grasped his firm length rising from the water like a reed in marshlands. She stroked a couple times then tugged firmly.

"I wondered when you'd get around to joining me," she said.

"You knew I was there?" he asked. Talking was hard for him. He had to thrash about to keep both of their heads out of the water—and she kept her grip on his lust-hard shaft.

"Of course I did, John. In fact, I've been waiting for you. Oh, how I have been waiting for you!"

The woman's auburn hair floated on the surface, forcing Slocum to toss his head to get it out of his face. As he did so he felt her tug him more firmly toward the spot he had been eyeing so avidly from the moment he saw her from the shore.

The purpled arrowhead of his manhood parted her nether lips and penetrated only an inch or so. The position of their bodies was all wrong, but for Slocum it felt as if lightning had struck him in the groin. The softness, the warmth and the curiously different wetness around the tip of his prod caused him to buck. But he wasn't able to thrust powerfully enough into her as they both desired.

"This'll take some rearranging," Ella declared. She moved lithely, slipping about in the water but never letting loose of the convenient handle she had found rising from the water. Tumbling about, sending up a spray that was sure to scare any fish in the pond, she maneuvered around until they were face to face.

"This is better," she said, kissing him. They bobbed up and down in the water, their bodies rubbing against one another. Slocum revelled in the feel of her breasts flattening against his broad, hairy chest almost as much as he enjoyed being able to stroke his hands up and down her smooth back to eventually cup her rounded moonlike rump.

He took a double handful and squeezed. Ella moaned softly and then kissed him with new passion. Her legs parted widely as she let him pull her body in close to his.

They fit together again like a tongue-and-groove furniture joint. Slocum sank deeper into her most intimate recess this time, the pressure from her female sheath bringing a gasp of delight to his lips.

"Like that, do you? Give me something to enjoy, too!" she taunted.

"You like it the way it is," he said. But his hands began kneading her rear end like lumps of pliant dough. As he pressed and pulled, squeezed and stroked, he felt her inner muscles responding of their own accord. He was pushing her desires to the breaking point. But he wanted more, and Ella did, too.

Bucking up and down, he began slipping in and out of her. The water robbed some of the slipperiness, but Slocum persevered, using short, quick strokes that caused the gorgeous woman to cry out in pleasure. They rolled over and over in the water, her legs wrapped around his waist. Slocum sputtered and so did Ella, but neither wanted to stop. In the middle of the limpid pool they continued their wild oscillations, striving and stroking, driving in and slipping away until Slocum was no longer able to control himself.

He felt her nipples harden and heard Ella's breathing turn staccato. Then his entire length was powerfully, delectably crushed as her inner muscles contracted in climax. He tried to maintain control to give her even more but found he could not do it. The burning tides rising within his loins could not be denied.

He erupted like a volcano.

Over and over they rolled in the water, until their passions were sated. Then Ella pushed away gently and once more floated on her back.

"This really won't do, you know," she said. Slocum paddled over beside her.

"What won't do?" he asked.

"I can hardly move my legs. You almost ripped me apart."

"Maybe I should kiss it and make it all better," Slocum suggested. He didn't wait to hear her elated acceptance of such a remedy before he dived down and came up between her parted thighs, his mouth applied fully to the fleecy triangle that still throbbed with need. His tongue lapped like a wave against a delightfully sexy shore until they were both ready again.

For a while, Slocum didn't care if he found the rustlers, because he had discovered paradise.

18

Slocum stretched out on the bank of the pond and felt the distant vibration coming up through the ground. He sat up in a hurry, dislodging Ella's head. She had been asleep, curled up next to him, her head on his shoulder.

"What's wrong?" she asked sleepily. She rolled over, rubbed her eyes and seemed unaware that she was still completely naked. Slocum had never seen a woman so sure of herself and her beauty—and so unconcerned about the effect it had on men.

"Wagon, probably, but it could be a few dozen cattle moving." Slocum dropped back and pressed his ear against a rocky patch a few feet away. He looked up. "Wagons. More than one."

"Those must be the ones from Kemmerer, the ones the professor ordered to haul his fossils."

Slocum watched the way her breasts jostled about in the warm afternoon sun, then forced his thoughts back to the matter at hand. He wanted to run the rustlers to ground and recover the Triple Cross cattle, and the wagons had nothing to do with that.

"Do get dressed, darling," Ella said, beginning the long process of climbing into her own clothing. Watching her move gracefully, shadows and light moving tantalizingly across bare white flesh, was enough to hold Slocum captive, but he shook off the desire to engage the woman yet another time.

"I need to escort the wagons to the dig," Ella said. "The professor was quite specific about that, since the canyon mouth on this side is not quite as obvious as at the other."

"And he didn't want Cope knowing the wagons were even on the way," Slocum guessed.

Ella laughed musically, tossed her long mane of auburn hair and fixed her bright sapphire eyes on him. "You understand the two of them all too well, John."

"They're both crazy as bedbugs," he said, settling his gunbelt around his waist. He was fully dressed now.

"Oh, not Othniel. He is an ambitious man, however. What do you think of the drawings I've done for him?" She pointed to a portfolio some distance away from the waterside. Slocum opened it and looked at the sepia ink drawings of various bones. He wasn't much of an art critic, unless the painting was of a provocatively naked woman and hung behind a bar.

"Nice," he said.

"Why, thank you for the feeble compliment," she said, diluting with a broad smile her displeasure at his lack of enthusiasm.

They fetched their horses and rode to the three wagons lumbering along at the far end of the large meadow.

"Howdy," called the driver of the lead wagon, not sure who he was greeting. "You the folks we was supposed to meet that'd lead us to the professor's camp?"

"I'm Ella Weedin," the auburn-haired woman called. "Professor Marsh sent me." She glanced at Slocum, and a small smile curled her lips. "And this is John Slocum."

"Slocum? The new foreman at the Triple Cross?" This recognition meant more to the driver than Ella's introduction. "Didn't know you was gonna be here, but I heard tell you was out here trackin' down them damned rustlers."

"You see any of them varmints?" Slocum asked. From the corner of his eye he saw Ella growing impatient at such pleasantries. She was as dedicated to digging the bones from the ground as either Marsh or Cope.

"Funny you should ask," the driver said. "Me and Cletus—he's back in the last wagon—we seen three fellows herdin' cattle. Didn't get a look at their faces and they wasn't any too friendly. Truth was, they tried to hide their ugly faces."

"Was one of them riding like he hurt?" asked Slocum.

"Kept clutchin' at his belly, now that you mention it. I thought he mighta et somethin' that didn't agree with him."

"Where'd you see him and the cattle?"

"John, please. The professor needs the supplies and you're holding up these men. Talk to them as we ride."

"I don't see the hurry," Slocum said, but he gave in to the woman's urging. He questioned the driver as they made their way through the winding canyons to Marsh's camp. When he had a good idea where the driver had spotted the rustlers, Slocum dropped back and spoke with the second driver and finally Cletus, bringing up the rear.

As he verified where they had last seen the outlaws herding a dozen head of cattle, Slocum saw that the corner of a tarp in Cletus's wagon had blown loose. Poking out from under the flapping edge he saw two crates of dynamite.

"You know what you're freighting?" Slocum asked.

Cletus nodded, looking as if he wanted to spit. "I'm the only one who's hauled dynamite before, so they put it in my wagon. There's enough to blow up an entire mountain."

Slocum considered what use Othniel Marsh might put it to. The rocky ground where he had made his find was slowly yielding its measure of dinosaur bones, and Slocum had heard the professor say that dynamite would only fracture what he wanted to save the most.

Or was it Edward Cope who had told him that?

"What're they going to use that much for?" Slocum asked, but he got only a sullen shrug as answer. He knew better than to press the teamster. Slocum considered what he ought to do, then put his heels to the Appaloosa's flanks and trotted up to where Ella rode, increasingly anxious to reach Marsh's excavation.

"I need to fetch the deputy," Slocum told her, "if I want to catch the rustlers. The drivers saw them at the far northern end of this valley, working a herd of stolen beeves."

"I'd hoped you would come to the camp and spend the night. It gets so lonely out here, John," she said in a sultry voice. Seeing that he wasn't going to accompany her, Ella shrugged, as if he meant nothing to her. "Do come by and see my new sketches sometime."

"I hope Marsh gets all those bones put together right," Slocum said, not sure what else to say to the woman. This time he was certain he was seeing her for the last time. They'd had their fun and it was best simply to ride off.

"It's Cope who can't assemble a skeleton properly," she said in a voice that might have come from Othniel Marsh's mouth.

"Goodbye, Ella," he said. She didn't bother responding. Ella Weedin was too busy directing the lead teamster into the proper canyon to deliver his supplies to Marsh before loading up the dinosaur skeletons for shipment back East.

Slocum drew rein, let the last wagon rattle past, then wheeled his Appaloosa and cantered back to the grassy meadow and beyond, to the twin-rutted trail left by the wagons. He stopped when he came to the place where Cletus and the lead driver had seen the rustlers in the distance. Slocum studied the lay of the land and tried to puzzle out the maze of canyons extending into the mountains at the far end of the valley.

A perfect place for hiding stolen cattle.

The paleontologists had probably driven the rustlers from their original camp. Moreover, now Marsh clawed away the very rock under the camp. With his crew, even stripped of the guards who had once worked for him, he presented a threat to the outlaws they dared not meet. Slocum's estimate had only four or five of the gang left in the saddle, and Blount was still hurting bad from the belly wound Slocum had inflicted.

They'd made their new hideout at the north end of the valley, but Slocum wasn't going to tangle with them alone. He had foolishly tried that before and nearly lost his life. It was time to get the deputy marshal from Kemmerer, as much as he hated to do that.

Slocum tugged on his reins and turned his horse's face. He had ridden for less than a half hour when he saw dust rising ahead along the trail. This wasn't a solitary rider, not from the amount of roiling brown kicked up into the air. Slocum had started for cover at the side of the trail when he realized the riders were coming too fast for him to hide.

Sunlight flashed off a half dozen rifle barrels—all pointed directly at him. Slocum halted and slowly raised his hands, grabbing a bit of sky and hoping the men wouldn't shoot him out of hand.

19

"No need to get itchy trigger fingers," Slocum called. He studied the men and decided none of them could hit him if he ducked, got his horse into a gallop and hightailed it back into the valley. But he didn't want to do that, since these were the very men he had been riding to Kemmerer to find.

"Lower those rifles, boys," Deputy Marshal Billy Gaines ordered. The lawman rode forward and holstered his six-shooter. "I ought to've knowed you'd be here, Slocum. You haven't been keepin' your nose clean, have you?"

"I just talked with the teamsters driving wagons over to Professor Marsh's camp," Slocum said, ignoring the deputy's dig at his character. "They spotted four or five men herding cattle stolen from the Triple Cross at the north end of this valley. I was on my way into town to tell you."

"Decided not to tangle with 'em all by your lonesome, eh?" Gaines laughed. "Ready to let experienced lawmen handle the crimes?"

Slocum glanced at Gaines's posse and wondered where those experienced peace officers might be. Gaines had

scavenged the Kemmerer saloons to find these men, probably offering them a dollar a day or all the whiskey they
could drink in an hour. As the wind shifted and Slocum
caught a whiff of the posse, he decided it was the latter.

"Arresting Blount will go a ways toward getting you
noticed by the marshal," Slocum said.

"That's not my intention," Gaines said, obviously lying.
He wanted the federal marshal's job so bad he could taste
it, but it wasn't right to let some drifter turned foreman
at the Triple Cross know of his ambitions. Slocum
couldn't have cared less what Gaines's motives were as
long as the deputy marshal did his duty and arrested
Blount, along with his gang.

"Let's ride. I scouted the spot from the trail about a
twenty-minute ride back." Slocum jerked his thumb in the
direction taken by Marsh's wagons.

"Come on, boys. Brace yourselves for some gunplay.
This might turn nasty real quick," Gaines warned. The
posse members muttered among themselves, but Slocum
gave them credit for not backing out now that arrests were
nigh.

As they rode, Slocum got to thinking about the dynamite in Cletus's wagon. He asked Gaines.

"Dynamite? I heard tell the little lady workin' for
Marsh ordered it. Made damn sure it was all there, too,
'fore it got freighted out here."

"Ella Weedin?"

Gaines leered. "That's the honey who was sweet on
you, Slocum. How could you forget? She was quite a
eyeful."

Slocum dismissed the deputy's continued fantasizing
about Ella and instead turned over in his mind her pur-
chase of the dynamite. He had no doubt that Professor
Marsh had authorized her to buy it. And he had no doubt
that Ella knew why the professor wanted so much explosive.

Slocum's speculation was cut short when one of the posse called, "There, Deputy, up there in the rocks!"

The words had hardly escaped his lips before all hell broke loose. The lookout spotted the posse at the same time they saw him. The sentry fired once, tried to cock his rifle again and lost his balance in his frantic haste. He slid on his butt across the rock, dropping his rifle as he fell. Crashing to the ground not ten feet from Slocum, the man lay flat on his back staring up at the sky with a dazed expression on his face. When he managed to focus his muddy brown eyes, he was staring down the barrel of Slocum's six-gun.

"Get that varmint hog-tied," the deputy ordered the man who had first spotted the guard. "Gag 'im, too. Don't want him lettin' the rest of the gang know we're a-comin' before we find 'em."

Slocum knew that hope had been dashed when the guard's rifle discharged. He looked to the deputy marshal for approval, then trotted straight down the rocky trail that entered yet another of the maze of canyons. From this juncture Slocum saw three branching trails, but he knew only one led to the rustlers—and they were not far away. There was no point posting a sentry a couple miles from their camp.

"Hear that?" Slocum asked Gaines.

"Cattle lowing. That way," the deputy said, pointing straight ahead.

"Wait," Slocum said. "Look at the other tracks. They're penning the stolen beeves ahead, but most of the horses' hoofprints show they're camped to the right."

Before the lawman responded, a bullet sailed past his ear. Billy Gaines ducked involuntarily, then cussed a blue streak. But in spite of his inventive cursing, he remained an easy target for the rustler.

Slocum located the shooter and got off a round at the rustler on foot a dozen yards away in a bramble thicket.

The man had been relieving himself when the posse rode up but now held a six-shooter in his hand. The rustler steadied his aim to take out the deputy marshal. At that range, he could not miss.

Slocum's quick second round caught the outlaw just under the throat and sent him stumbling back, dead before he hit the ground.

"Two down," Gaines said, wiping sweat from his forehead as he stared at the body. "You saved my bacon, for sure, Slocum. Thanks. I owe you. You reckon there're as many as three left?"

"Might be more. I don't have any idea if I've seen them all at one time, but I do know there's going to be one I want."

"Blount," Gaines said. "You don't go killin' him for nuthin', Slocum. If you can, you gotta let him live to stand trial."

Slocum had tried that once. He wouldn't make the same mistake twice. He put his heels to his Appaloosa and started up the canyon toward the outlaw camp. He didn't get ten yards before he saw how Blount had set up his camp. Small caves along the walls afforded decent shelter; small cooking fires burned in front of two of the depressions.

"I don't wanta chase any of 'em into a cave," Gaines grumbled. "I'll get some of that dynamite over in Marsh's camp and seal 'em up, I swear I will!"

Slocum was more worried about staying alive. Two other rustlers came from the caves, rifles blazing. One slug whined past his ear. Slocum didn't have to look behind him to know the bullet that had missed him had found a target in another of the posse. From the way the deputized lawman whined and moaned, it wasn't serious, but it reduced their firepower by one.

Slocum fired twice more and his six-shooter came up empty. Rather than pulling back to reload or to swing his

Winchester into action, Slocum bent low and urged the Appaloosa straight ahead so he could ride down the outlaw. The man stood, staring at Slocum in surprise since he had thought his attacker would turn tail and find a safe place to reload.

Diving from horseback, Slocum crashed into the rustler and crushed him to the ground. The impact shook Slocum, but it knocked the wind from the outlaw's lungs. He lay on the ground vainly gasping for breath. Slocum didn't give him a chance to recover. Judging his distance, he reared back and swung his Colt Navy. The blued steel barrel landed alongside the man's head.

"We got the rest of 'em. Good work, boys!" shouted Deputy Gaines.

"Where's Blount?" asked Slocum. He stood and looked around the camp, doing a quick inventory. There was one too many bedrolls stretched in the shallow caves.

"Don't see him."

"Where do they corral their horses?" Slocum asked. He made a full circle hunting for the rustlers' mounts. He stopped when he saw that tracks led deeper into the canyon, around a bend. Quickly reloading his six-gun, Slocum grabbed the reins of his Appaloosa and swung into the saddle again.

"He might not have been in camp, Slocum," Gaines said.

"He was here," Slocum said grimly. "I can smell him."

Gaines looked strangely at Slocum, then nodded. Slocum started for the far side of the rustlers' camp.

"You want help?" asked Gaines. This surprised Slocum. He stared at the deputy marshal, who explained, "I reckon I owe you somethin' for takin' down that other son of a bitch 'fore he ventilated me. Bring Blount back, Slocum. I don't much care how."

"Thanks," Slocum said, his mind now entirely on finding Blount. He rounded a sharp bend and saw where the rustlers had their corral. A quick count showed one horse missing. When the posse had ridden into camp, Blount had been here tending his horse. Or maybe he had a bump on his head that itched when the law got too close. It didn't matter to Slocum why Blount had lit out.

He rode after him, occasionally studying the rocky ground for any sign that the outlaw was slowing. For more than a mile into the canyon Blount's tracks showed he was pushing his horse to exhaustion. Slocum grew wary because he knew he would overtake the rustler at any minute after his quarry's horse tired.

And he did.

Ahead, in the middle of the canyon, on foot and tugging hard on his horse's bridle, Blount struggled to get away. When he saw Slocum riding up behind him, he snarled and went for his six-shooter.

Slocum ignored the slugs whipping past and concentrated only on the outlaw. Blount was growing frantic, but he had ridden away better prepared than Slocum would have thought. When Blount's six-shooter came up empty, he grabbed for his saddlebags and drew out another gun. He kept flinging lead in Slocum's direction.

Only when one round bit a bloody chunk out of Slocum's left ear did he draw his own pistol and level it.

"How do you want to do this, Blount?" Slocum called. "You want to go back over your horse or riding it?"

"Go to hell!" Blount emptied this gun and grabbed for a box of cartridges in his saddlebags. He abandoned his horse and ran clumsily for cover. Slocum measured each round he fired, but Blount's uneven gait saved him. The outlaw's earlier belly wound prevented him from running easily and threw off Slocum's aim.

"Have it your way," Slocum said, jumping to the ground. He grabbed his rifle from the saddle sheath and swatted his Appaloosa on the rump. The horse let out an aggrieved snort and raced away. Slocum took his time picking a spot for the fight. He didn't want the exchange to last long.

"I'll kill you. Why couldn't you leave me be?" demanded Blount. He poked his head above the rock where he had taken shelter and loosed a hail of bullets. Slocum counted five rounds, but the outlaw might have reloaded his other six-gun. Any mistake now meant Slocum's death.

Therefore, he had to wait for Blount to make the mistake.

"That belly wound hurting you, Blount?" Slocum taunted. "Or maybe the right arm? That ever start to heal? Can you hang on to a gun properly?"

"You won't get away with shooting me the way you did," Blount screamed. Slocum knew the outlaw was nearing the end of his rope. He levered a round into the Winchester's chamber, rested the forward stock in the palm of his left hand and braced himself against a rock. Then he waited.

During the war Slocum had been a sniper and a good one, to boot. Sitting in a tree all day waiting for the flash of sunlight off a Yankee officer's gold braid was all he did. Cut off the head and the body flopped around like a chicken. More than one battle had been turned in the CSA's favor by Slocum's accurate shooting.

"You run off? You turnin' lily-livered, you stinkin' coward?" No matter how Blount ranted, Slocum remained calm.

Slocum used the time to reflect on all Blount had done. The rustler was responsible for Chafee's death and the theft of a small herd from the Triple Cross. He had almost killed Slocum with a dynamite charge on the canyon rim, and Slocum's jaw was still sore from the mule's kick Blount had given him when he escaped.

Slocum remembered sighting down the barrel of a six-shooter and having his hammer fall on a spent chamber.

He remembered how he had decided to take Blount in to Kemmerer for trial.

The leader of the rustlers poked his head up so he could get a glimpse of Slocum. Slocum's finger drew back slowly, and his Winchester bucked hard against his shoulder.

He didn't have to go see that he had hit Blount smack dab between the eyes. He felt it, as he had any number of kills he'd made before.

Slocum sat back on his haunches, took a deep breath, wiped away sweat formed by the tension of waiting, then stood and walked cautiously to where the outlaw lay sprawled on his back. Blount stared sightlessly at nothing, a six-shooter clutched in one hand and the other spilling out a half dozen cartridges he had intended to use for reloading.

He wouldn't have to worry about his six-shooter coming up empty again. Ever.

20

"We can leave the cattle here for a spell, Deputy," Slocum said. Gaines intended to drive more than eighty head of stolen beeves from the canyon, through the high meadow and out onto the grasslands, where Triple Cross cowboys could take them back to their proper range.

"Don't worry your head on it, Slocum," Gaines said. "The people of Wyoming owe you a lot. You stopped a vicious ring of rustlers, almost by yourself." Gaines coughed and looked at Slocum from the corner of his eye. "Of course, you couldn't have done it without proper support from the federal marshal's office."

"Of course not," Slocum said dryly. He didn't care if Gaines took the credit—and the reward—for capturing the outlaws. All Slocum had set out to do was avenge Chafee's death and to get the cattle back where they belonged. It would certainly please Mr. Mathiesen seeing almost two thousand dollars' worth of cattle on his range again, since this might be the difference between a profit or a loss for the entire year.

"Sorry I mistook you for one of the bad guys," Gaines went on, obviously struggling to find words to apologize to Slocum for having arrested him earlier. "Here's the bail money the professor put up for you." Gaines fished about in his pocket and pulled out a sweat-soaked wad of greenbacks drawn on a Cheyenne bank, rather than the gold coins Othniel Marsh had given him originally.

Slocum reached over and took the bills.

"Thanks," he said. "I reckon I ought to give this back to the professor. But why're you giving the money to me instead of taking it directly to Marsh?"

"From the way that artist lady looked at you, you probably have more reason to go there than I do."

The deputy marshal paid what he owed. Slocum snorted. He and Ella were good together, but they had probably come to the end of their trail. That was something he couldn't quite decide. But the truth was, he wouldn't mind seeing her again, and returning the money gave him a decent excuse.

"Hey, Mr. Slocum!" came the shout from ahead. "That you? You and the deputy from up north?"

"That's Tatum," Slocum said to the deputy marshal.

"Enthusiastic cuss, ain't he?"

Slocum waited for Tatum and another hand named Sizemore from the Triple Cross to gallop up, their horses roiling the dust to the choking point.

"You found 'em. This is gonna lift Mr. Mathiesen's spirits to the sky, Mr. Slocum."

"Me and Slocum found them," Gaines cut in, wanting witnesses so he could claim whatever reward there might be. "Captured the whole gang, the ones that didn't buy themselves a piece of real estate."

Tatum's eyes went saucer-wide as he looked from the deputy to Slocum and back.

"They're gonna be talkin' on this for years. A whole gang of rustlers and you got back our cattle."

"Some of them," Slocum said. "We need to find out who was buying the stolen beeves and put them out of business, too." He looked significantly at Deputy Gaines.

"That'll be a feather in anyone's cap, breaking up a gang of rustlers operating throughout the entire territory."

"I got men lookin' into it," Billy Gaines lied, but Slocum saw the determined set to the deputy's jaw and knew he would carry out the rest of the investigation until the men buying and transporting the stolen cattle were in cells adjoining those occupied by the rustlers they had caught.

"Tatum, why don't you and Sizemore there drive the cattle back to the pastureland just east of the ranch house?"

"Mr. Mathiesen'll want to throw you the finest goldurned party you ever did see. When'll you be back, Mr. Slocum?"

"Not long," he said, wondering if that might be so.

"Well, we surely do need you. There's been some more dynamite stolen."

Slocum fixed his steely gaze on Tatum.

"Last night," the young man went on. "Took every stick of the dynamite we bought to replace what them rustlers took."

"There wasn't any dynamite in the rustlers' camp," Gaines said. "I searched everything they had, figurin' I might get back other stolen property."

"I think I know who took it," Slocum said, remembering the cases of explosive in the wagon bound for Othniel Marsh's camp. If one scientist had it, so would the other—and for the same reason. They each might have what they called the find of the century, but their profession and personal animosity was too great.

With so much dynamite in their hands, Marsh and Cope might blow up half of Wyoming.

"I'll see to it," Slocum said, coming to a decision. Getting involved was foolish, but he had to do what he could to stop the men from escalating their animosity to the point where dozens could die.

"If somethin's been stole, I should—" Gaines cut off

his declaration of duty when he saw the grim expression on Slocum's face.

"I'll be along shortly," Slocum told Tatum. He nodded in the deputy marshal's direction and then rode back into the valley, heading for the canyon mouth that would lead him into Marsh's camp. As he rode, his mind raced. He couldn't come to any good decision how to proceed if both camps intended using dynamite on each other. The distance to the excavation site seemed like a few hundred yards, rather than the miles it was, due to his inability to figure out a plan to wrest the explosives from the two scientists.

He entered Marsh's camp, looking around for Ella Weedin, but he didn't see her anywhere.

"Mr. Slocum!" called the professor, bustling over and fussing at his clothing. He looked perturbed, and Slocum thought he knew why.

"The deputy marshal's returned the money you posted for my bail," Slocum said, handing over the thick roll of greenbacks. He didn't bother dismounting.

"That's, uh, that is mighty fine of him. I had not expected it." Marsh looked over his shoulder, back down the canyon in the direction of Cope's dig.

"While I'm here, I came to pay my respects to Miss Weedin."

"She's not here," Marsh said too quickly. Slocum remembered what the wagon driver had said about who had bought the dynamite. Marsh knew, but that had been Ella's order rattling about in the back of the wagon. He might have paid for the explosives, but Slocum knew now the dynamite was all the auburn-haired woman's doing.

A distant clap of thunder rumbled. Slocum looked up to the sky and saw leaden clouds building over the distant, rocky canyon rims.

"Mighty big storm coming," he told the professor. "You'll want to get to higher ground till after it's passed."

"I have two wagons filled with bones ready to be shipped. I'm hurrying with the third."

Another deep rumble reverberated down the canyon. Slocum didn't think this one came from a thunderstorm. He wondered how long it would be until Edward Cope retaliated with the dynamite he had stolen from the Triple Cross.

Slocum decided he didn't want to know. Let the academics blow themselves to hell and gone, with Ella's help. He had wanted to see Ella again, but not if she was involved in planting dynamite that would not only destroy the other paleontologist's fossils but possibly also take his life. She was dutifully wrapped up in a feud that went beyond the bounds of sanity.

But weren't all feuds crazy?

Slocum touched the brim of his hat, wished the professor a good day and then trotted from the excavation site. The Triple Cross needed him, at least until they drove the cattle to market, and another of Mrs. Mathiesen's fine meals would be just the medicine he needed to get the bad taste out of his mouth.

Watch for
SLOCUM AND THE STOREKEEPER'S WIFE

**300th novel in the exciting SLOCUM series
from Jove**

Coming in February!

LONGARM

**Explore the exciting Old West with one
of the men who made it wild!**